D0435438

3 1984

J   **Collier, James Lincoln.**
       Planet out of the past. New York, Macmillan, c1983.
       162 p. 22 cm.

       Summary: Young people search for hominids on another planet similar to Earth and experience all the dangers Earth possessed in prehistoric times.

     1. Man, Prehistoric—Fiction. 2. Science fiction. I. Title.

PLANET OUT OF THE PAST

PLANET
OUT OF THE PAST

JAMES LINCOLN COLLIER

MACMILLAN PUBLISHING COMPANY
NEW YORK

COLLIER MACMILLAN PUBLISHERS
LONDON

Copyright © 1983 James Lincoln Collier
All rights reserved. No part of this book may be reproduced
or transmitted in any form or by any means, electronic or
mechanical, including photocopying, recording or by any
information storage and retrieval system, without
permission in writing from the Publisher.

Macmillan Publishing Company
866 Third Avenue, New York, N.Y. 10022
Collier Macmillan Canada, Inc.

Printed in the United States of America
10 9 8 7 6 5 4 3 2 1

Library of Congress Cataloging in Publication Data
Collier, James Lincoln, date.
Planet out of the past.

Summary: Young people search for hominids on another
planet similar to Earth and experience all the dangers
Earth possessed in prehistoric times.
[1. Man, Prehistoric—Fiction.   2. Science fiction]
I. Title.
PZ7.C678Pl   1983   [Fic]   83-9365
ISBN 0-02-722860-6

FOR LYDIA AND JAMIE

1.

"Do you think he got killed?" Weddy said.

"No," I said. "I don't think so." But I wasn't so sure. Professor Joher hadn't taken anything but his specimen knife with him when he'd gone off in the morning. He was only going for a short look around, he'd said. Now it was six hours later. I knew that there were plenty of animals on this strange planet that'd kill him if they got the chance. Saber-toothed tigers, for one. But I didn't want to worry Weddy or Nuell. "I think he just got lost," I said.

"How could he have gotten lost?" Nuell said. "All you have to do is climb one of those tall trees and you'd be able to see the spaceship from miles away." He pointed to one of the acacia trees that dotted the plain around us.

It was true, but I didn't want to admit it to them. "I still think he's okay. You know what he's like. Once he gets to concentrating on something he completely forgets about time."

"Still," Weddy said, "I'm worried. I think we should go look for him."

"Let me think a minute," I said. I was pretty worried myself. For one thing, if anything happened to Professor Joher, I wasn't sure that I could fly the spaceship back to earth myself. The professor had gone over the controls with me, but he hadn't given me much chance to practice. Professor Joher was only interested in one thing—the ancient types of men he hoped we'd find on the new planet, and he didn't want to bother with anything else. But of course it wasn't just flying the spaceship. Professor Joher was Weddy and Nuell's father. He was my father, too, in a way, but of course I'd never tell them I felt like that. We had to find him. "The big question is whether one of us ought to stay with the spaceship."

"Come on, Char," Nuell said. "Let's stop standing around. Let's get going while his track is still fresh." He stooped, picked up a stone and began tossing it from hand to hand, whistling tonelessly at the same time.

I frowned. "How can I think when you're doing that, Nuell?"

Nuell gave me a look. "Stop trying to tell everybody what to do, Char," he said.

I didn't say anything. Nuell never liked my being boss, because he was almost my age. But Nuell was always dashing into things and messing them up, and I knew that Professor Joher counted on me to think things through and be sensible. So it was up to me to take charge, whether Nuell liked it or not. "Nuell, you're making me crazy throwing that stone around like that," I said.

"Will you two please stop arguing?" Weddy said.

Nuell gave her a look, too. Then he wandered around to the other side of the spaceship. "Still, Char," Weddy said, "we ought to get going while the trail's fresh."

The funny thing was, I was sick and tired of having to take charge. All my life, it seemed, I'd had to take care of things for everybody. It wasn't any fun. I was fed up with it. "I think we'd better all go," I said. The problem was that if the professor was hurt or something, it would take the three of us to carry him back to the spaceship. I looked around. The sun on the plain was baking hot, and we were standing in the shade of the spaceship. The plain rolled away from us toward white-capped volcanic mountains in the distance. Out in the tall savannah grass, among the acacia trees, were herds of odd animals—tiny three-toed horses, pigs three feet high at the shoulder, elephants with upside-down tusks that curved to the ground. Among them, I knew, were a dozen different kinds of predatory cats—jaguars, leopards, the enormous saber-toothed *Smilodon*. An unarmed man would be easy meat for any of those cats.

Suddenly, we heard Nuell shout: "Hey, you guys, take a look at this." We dashed around to the sunny side of the spaceship. Nuell was pointing out toward the tall, gray green grass. There, moving in a loose pack, were six or seven of the biggest primates I'd ever seen. "Some kind of gorillas," Nuell said.

"Quick, the viewing screen," I said. We raced back around the spaceship and scrambled up the ladder into the control room. I snapped on the viewing screen and dialed the controls. In a few seconds I had them focused and brought them in close.

"Wow," Weddy said.

They were knuckle-walking the way gorillas do, with their bodies tilted up at an angle and their arms acting as front legs. But they were a lot bigger than any modern gorilla. I figured they must be over six feet tall when they stood straight up and they had jaws so enormous they looked like they could crush rocks.

"Look at those jaws," Weddy said. "What are they?"

It made me glad when she asked me some question like that. Nuell wouldn't know the answer. "*Gigantopithecus*, probably," I said. "They must weigh five hundred pounds. Being as big as that, they need to eat an awful lot of vegetation every day to keep going. Grass and leaves, probably. Fruit, if they can find it. They need huge jaws like that to chew it up."

"They look pretty scary," Weddy said.

I shook my head. "I doubt if they're dangerous. They wouldn't be meat eaters, so they wouldn't hurt. I mean if you started something with them they'd go for you, but I think if you left them alone they wouldn't bother you. The only primate that hunts is the human being."

"And makes war," Weddy said.

That wasn't exactly true, I knew: Chimpanzees fight wars sometimes. But I didn't want to get into it just then. "These aren't really hominids," I said. "They're pithecines—ape types."

"We don't even know if there are any hominids on Pleisto," Weddy said. "Nobody's seen any yet."

"Dad thinks there are," Nuell said.

"Let's not argue it now," I said. "I think we'd better all go after your father. Let's grab the electro-prods and get out of here."

Now I wished that the Research Committee had let us bring better weapons to Pleisto. The electro-prods were okay for fending off smaller animals, maybe even jaguars. But they weren't going to be much use against a herd of *Deinotherium*, say, those huge elephants with the upside-down tusks. But the Committee had been so worried about explorers killing anything and messing up the ecology of Pleisto before it got carefully studied that they wouldn't let us take anything but the prods—just six-foot steel rods that telescoped back into their generating packs.

We climbed down out of the spaceship and started off in the direction Professor Joher had gone that morning. We could still make out his track through the savannah grass. It wasn't much of a track, though. Most of the grass he'd trampled down had sprung back, but here and there we could make out broken stems, or scuff marks in the dirt beneath the grass. We walked three abreast about ten feet apart to make sure we didn't miss any signs of him.

It was hot and we started to sweat quickly. We weren't making very good time and for an hour there was nothing. At some places the track was clear and a couple of feet wide, and we could guess that here the professor had gone down on his hands and knees and crawled for a while, maybe trying to follow some kind of trail in the grass. At other places his track practically disappeared and we knew that he'd gotten up and walked, or even run, with that long-legged stride he had. When he was moving like that his trail practically disappeared—just a broken stem here and there. It was pretty discouraging because if he were going at any speed he'd be getting farther away from us every minute. Finally, we stopped and rested in the shade of an acacia tree, crouched on our haunches. "He obviously was following something on the ground," I said. "The trail of a small animal, maybe."

Nuell shook his head. "Ducking," he said.

"Ducking?"

"Sure," Nuell said. "He was following something,

and every once in a while he'd get too close and worry that they'd spot him. So he'd duck down and crawl along the ground."

It was a good idea and I wished I'd thought of it first. I gave Weddy a quick look. "If it were something he might scare off he'd have gone on his hands and knees the whole time."

"Not if they were going along pretty fast and kept looking around all the time. When they got over a hill or around a piece of woods he'd have to run to keep them in sight and then he'd have to go on his hands and knees again."

Nuell was right. I felt outsmarted, but I knew I'd just look stupid if I went on arguing about it. I gave Weddy another look, but she was looking at Nuell. "What kind of animals would be going that fast?" I said.

"*Elephas*, maybe. Or those pygmy giraffes we saw yesterday."

I didn't think it was either of these. Elephas were elephant types with long, thin heads. They wouldn't be dangerous and neither would pygmy giraffes. They were browsers, eating leaves and grass, and would be moving slowly across the plains. I was pretty sure that Professor Joher had been following something more dangerous. But what? And had they got him in the end? I'd seen the bodies of baboons rotting in the crotches of trees where jaguars had left them for safekeeping. I shuddered. Could the professor be stuck in some tree, half-eaten, his face gnawed, his stomach ripped open?

Suddenly, a great feeling of loneliness came over me. For the past five years, since I'd left home and come to live with the Johers, the professor had always been there, somebody I could count on to take care of things when something went wrong. It had been the first time in my life I'd ever had somebody like that; always before, even when I was just a little kid, everything had depended on me. Now the professor was gone, and it was all on me again. The loneliness filled me like cold water. It scared me and I wanted to curl up in the grass and sleep. But it was all up to me. "Let's get going," I said.

We started following the trail again. Ahead of us was a patch of thorny acacia woods. It looked to be about a quarter of a mile on a side and there was sparse brush growing underneath. The trail led right for it. We tracked it to the edge of the woods. Then we stopped dead. There at the edge of the shadows of the woods was a big patch of trampled grass about fifteen feet across. Lying at one corner of the area was a white cloth hat with a green visor.

We dashed toward it. "Don't touch it," I said. If there were any clues there we shouldn't disturb them. We bent over it. There was a tear in one side of the crown and around the tear was a smudge of dirt.

We stared at it, not saying anything. My heart was thumping. Finally, Nuell straightened up and glanced around the savannah as if he expected to see something there. "Something got Dad," he said. His face was white.

Weddy was pale, too. "I don't believe it," she said. "He's too smart. He's too smart for anything on this planet."

I knew what she was feeling, because I was feeling it, too. Professor Joher always seemed so strong, so sure of himself. It just didn't seem possible for anything to happen to him. But still, there was his hat. "Let's not jump to conclusions," I said. "We don't know anything for sure yet. Let's have a good look around." The three of us bent and began moving slowly around to search the area.

In a minute Weddy said, "Look. Blood." Nuell and I ran over to her. A trail of tiny red dots went across the crushed grass into the woods.

"I told you something got him," Nuell said. His face was still white and his fists were clenched at his sides as if somehow by hitting something he could solve the problem. Suddenly, he swung around to face me. "We should have started sooner, Char," he shouted. "I told you, we shouldn't have waited."

Why was it my fault? "Listen, Nuell—"

"Stop it, you two," Weddy said sharply. "Stop it. We have to find Dad."

I was still angry at Nuell, but I took a deep breath and calmed myself down. "We have to stop jumping to conclusions," I said. "We don't know if that's his blood. Maybe something attacked him and he wounded it with his specimen knife."

"What about the hat?" Nuell demanded. His fists

were still clenched at his sides. "How did it get that tear?"

"Calm down, Nuell," Weddy said. "Don't blame it on Char. It isn't his fault."

"We should have left sooner," he said. "We shouldn't have wasted so much time. That blood is fresh. It only happened a little while ago."

"Nuell," I said, "I told you—maybe it isn't your dad's blood." Why was Nuell blaming it on me? He's my dad, too, I thought—almost.

Nuell shook his arms as if he wanted to hit something again, and then his fists unclenched. "All right. What are we going to do?"

"Let's see where the blood goes." We trotted to the edge of the woods and looked into the shadows. There were no more signs of blood. We came back out and crouched around the hat.

"He must have been hit," Nuell said. "Look at that tear."

Crouching over the hat, I remembered that a scientist, especially one whose job is digging up old bones, never moves anything until he's examined it carefully. I knew I should be looking for clues around the hat, but I couldn't think of what kind of clues to look for. Finally, I picked the hat up. We stood and they gathered around me, staring at it. The tear near the crown was about an inch long and the smudge around it was brownish. It seemed pretty clear that something had attacked him, all right. But I didn't want to believe it and anyway, it was my job to keep things hopeful. "It could have been almost anything. Maybe he tripped and the hat fell off and he stepped on it. Or he banged into a branch going into the woods. Anything."

"Not a branch," Nuell said. "How could a branch make a rip like that?"

"It's possible," I said. But it wasn't.

"I don't think so, either," Weddy said. "It would have to be something sharp. A fang or a claw."

"No," Nuell said. "Not a fang or a claw, either. They'd rip, but they wouldn't leave a smudge like that."

"Maybe the dirt was already there," I said. "The tear just happened there by accident."

We were all scared. My face felt clammy, and I could see the clamminess on the others' faces, too. "Listen," Weddy said. "If Dad were hurt, he might be right around here somewhere. Let's find him."

"A tusk," Nuell said suddenly. "Or a hoof. That would explain the dirt smudge."

It was a smart idea, and better than that, it meant that he might not have been hurt so badly. "Maybe," I said.

"Come on, let's go find him," Weddy said. "He may be lying there bleeding."

"Not if he had been kicked," I said. "If it were that, it wouldn't be so bad. He could have startled a mother zebra or something lying in the tall grass with her newborn. She'd have jumped and kicked."

"Then where is he?" Nuell demanded.

"He'd have crawled off into the woods to get away," I said.

"Let's find him," Weddy insisted.

We spread out again and walked into the shadowy woods. Under the tall acacias the undergrowth was thin and there were grassy patches. We wouldn't have much trouble spotting the professor if he were lying some-where. We went through the woods and came out the other side and then we turned, moved along twenty yards and went back through the other way. We were almost out the side we'd come in when Nuell saw more blood. This time it wasn't drops, but a fair-sized splash several inches in diameter, with a trail dwindling away from it. We bent over it and then we saw the stone. It was a little smaller than a tennis ball. One half of it was round and smooth—I figured that it probably had lain in a stream bed for thousands of years and had been worn down that way. But the thing that made the chill go right up my back was the way the other side was rough. It had been chipped away to form a cutting edge —rough, but good enough for hacking through the skin of a zebra or antelope. I knew instantly that it had been made by a human being.

2.

Of course, we weren't supposed to be on Pleisto all by ourselves—just Weddy, Nuell, Professor Joher and me. We'd come as Professor Joher's student assistants in the little spaceship. The main exploration team—twenty people from various branches of the sciences—had come in the big spaceship. But halfway out to Pleisto the rockets on the big ship began acting up and they'd had to turn back for earth or risk floating endlessly through empty space for the rest of their lives. So we had gone on alone.

The Committee hadn't really wanted us to do it. They'd suggested that we turn back, too. But the professor had been afraid that if we turned back he'd never get this great opportunity again. He'd argued with the Committee, saying that it would be a terrible waste of money for us to turn back, and finally they said we could go ahead.

Professor Joher was right about one thing: Coming out to Pleisto was a tremendous opportunity for him—the chance of a lifetime to find the answers to some of the big questions scientists had been asking about human life for centuries. Pleisto had only been discovered a decade before. It was one of three planets circling a sun called K27. Nobody had ever paid much attention to the K27 solar system. It was small and far away, and astronomers were a lot more interested in black holes and such. But then some young astrophysicist started to chart that area of the universe just for practice. He discovered that Pleisto was a lot like the earth in size and distance from its sun. He checked some more and found out that Pleisto also had a mineral content and an atmosphere almost identical to the earth's. Of course, when that came out it caused a huge stir. Everybody wanted to visit Pleisto—geologists, botanists, zoologists, you name it.

So the Committee was formed and scientists began to go. They discovered immediately what they suspected they'd find—that there was life on Pleisto. Once this came out the Committee set up very strict rules about how everything was to be done. Basically, they were scared that humans would bring in bacteria that could kill off whole populations of animals or vegetation. Or maybe exudes from the spaceships would unbalance the atmosphere. Or the presence of humans would scare animals out of their natural habitats and cause changes in the ecological system. We'd seen it happen on earth often enough when some chemical pollution would kill off the algae in a lake. The little fish that depended on the algae would die off; after that, the big fish that ate the little fish would go, and then the diving birds that ate the big fish and the snakes that ate the birds' eggs— one by one they'd go, too, until the lake was just dead water.

Anyway, the Committee was cautious and explorations went along slowly. But after the first five years, just about the time I was starting in with Professor Joher, we could tell pretty well that Pleisto was almost a replica of the earth as it had been in Pleistocene times, about two million years ago. Oh, it wasn't all the same. Pleisto rotated on its axis a little more slowly than the earth, so that it had a thirty-three-hour day, with the nights colder and the days hotter. Its circuit around the sun was longer, too, taking nearly five hundred of its days, so that the seasons were longer. But it was just amazing how much Pleisto was like the earth in most ways. It meant that going out to Pleisto was like going back into the earth's past. You could actually see and touch the world of two million years ago.

And, of course, Professor Joher was crazy to go. He'd spent all of his life studying ancient men—the early hominids that modern humans are descended from. I guess he was recognized as one of the top people in his field. But all of his study had been done from fossil bones, from stone tools, from examining the refuse in million-year-old campsites where ancient men had once hunted, fished, butchered their kills, lived and died.

And the big question was: Were there any examples of ancient hominids—so-called "cave men"—still alive on Pleisto? The first explorers found no trace of them. But that wouldn't satisfy the professor. They were mostly geologists, chemists, botanists. Only somebody who really knew how ancient people lived would know where to look for them and how to spot the signs that they were there. For three years Professor Joher begged the Committee to let him go, and finally they said he could. And now, after we'd been on Pleisto for only two days, the professor was gone and maybe dead, and we were standing over the little patch of dried blood, holding in our hands a stone tool that had been made by somebody human.

Despite everything, it thrilled me just to hold that piece of rock in my hand. It was, I knew, one of the most important discoveries ever made in the science of man. Only a few hours before, that stone had been touched by a member of another species of human beings—an ancient ancestor with a smaller brain than mine, and maybe a hairier body, but somebody who was human all the same.

"What is it exactly, Char?" Weddy asked.

"A bifacial quartzite chopper," I said. "See, they knocked pieces of stone off two sides to make a rough edge." I felt the edge with my finger. "It's pretty sharp. Sharp enough to cut up an animal."

"It was a butchering tool, then," she said.

"Probably," I said. "Of course, nobody's ever known for sure, at least until now, exactly how these old tools were used. But that's the idea. When human beings first began to eat a lot of meat, instead of vegetation, the biggest problem wasn't so much hunting, but cutting the animals up afterward, especially cutting through the skin. They didn't have fangs or claws, so they began to make tools."

"So that's what punched the hole in Dad's hat," Nuell said. "Did they throw it, or what, Char?"

I shrugged. "I don't know. But I guess we'll find out sooner or later."

"But what did they do with Dad?" Weddy asked. "Do you think they killed him?"

"No," I said. But I was just saying that to be optimistic. They could easily have killed him. Worse than that, they could have butchered him and eaten him. The idea made me shudder. There were, in Pleistocene times, a whole group of ape-men types—some more to the ape side, some more human—and the chances were pretty good that they preyed on each other for food. Professor Joher was of a different species from whoever had got him. They'd be as likely to see him as food as a smilodon would.

Yet maybe not. If they'd killed him for food they'd

almost certainly have cut him up on the spot and carried the parts they wanted back to wherever they were camped. There'd have been a lot of flesh and blood and bones strewn around. There wasn't any sign of that. I didn't want to say this to Weddy and Nuell, though. He was their father. "I think they must have taken him prisoner," I said. "If he'd been killed, there'd be more signs of it."

"I think so, too," Nuell said. "They would want to know about him. They would be curious about us. See, what I figure is that they've been hanging around spying on us ever since we came down."

"Why would they do that?" Weddy said. "I think they'd have been scared of the spaceship and run away."

"They might have been scared, but they'd have hung around all the same," Nuell said. "If some strange thing came flying down into your backyard and a lot of funny-looking people got out, you'd want to know what they were up to, wouldn't you? You wouldn't just run away, you'd put out spies."

I wasn't so sure. Nuell was a lazy student. He'd always preferred playing skate ball to poring over fossil bones in the laboratory. It was risky to assume that an ancient hominid would think the way modern humans did. They might, and then again they might not. But I didn't want to discourage the idea that the professor had been taken prisoner. "They might have," I said.

"They must have, Char," Nuell said. "Then this morning Dad spotted them and started to follow them.

He didn't want to lost track of them, so he couldn't come back to the spaceship to get us. He just followed after them, ducking down when they looked around. Probably he figured they'd lead him to their campsite, and then he could come back for us. But they saw him and hid at the edge of the woods and ambushed him."

It was a pretty good theory, I realized. Nuell was hasty about things; he didn't stop to think a lot of times. But sometimes he would see things that the rest of us would miss—his mind would sort of skip to the right conclusion without getting there step by step. Sometimes I wondered what Professor Joher thought of Nuell. Was he disappointed that Nuell was not much of a scholar? Did he think that someday Nuell would steady down and dig into his studies? Or did he really notice at all? And how did he feel about the fact that I was the best student of the three of us? "You might be right, Nuell," I said.

"It has to be right," he said impatiently. "Come on, let's get going before they get too far away."

What we all realized without saying it, was that if the creatures—whatever they were—had spotted Professor Joher, they might have spotted us, too. We all felt some unseen presence, maybe only a few yards away, watching us—perhaps waiting to pounce on us as they had on the professor.

We moved out of the woods and, at what on earth would have been the northwest side of the woods, we found the trail. It was a much broader, more obvious trail than the one the professor had left by himself. "There must have been a bunch of them," Nuell said.

"Two or three at least," I said. I crouched over the track of bent and broken grass, hoping I'd find footprints. In the laboratory we'd reconstructed hominid feet from fossil bones, and I had a pretty good idea what kinds of prints the various types of hominids would leave. But there were no footprints. The dirt was too hard. I was disappointed.

"Let's go," Nuell said impatiently once again.

I rose up and stared around. "Take it easy, Nuell," I said. "We don't want to walk into an ambush. I think one of us better walk out ahead to act as a scout. We'll take turns."

"I'll go first," Nuell said. He turned and started to trot off along the broad trail left by the hominids.

"Nuell," I called. "Take it slow. There's no rush. They'll be heading for a campsite somewhere. We'll catch up to them sooner or later."

He realized that he was being foolish. He slowed his pace, looking left and right, and when he'd gotten fifty yards out into the savannah grass, Weddy and I began to follow after him. I glanced at Weddy walking along beside me. She wasn't so white any more, but her face was serious and her lips tight. I knew that inside her body her heart was racing and she was scared. I wanted to put my arm around her and hug her, but I didn't dare. I just kept on walking.

The landscape we were going through was pretty

much like what we'd come through already. The tall grass rolled like a sea across low hills to the distant mountains at the end of the view. Everywhere there were acacia trees, sometimes standing tall and alone, sometimes in patches, like islands in the sea. And everywhere, too, there were animals: herds of pygmy giraffes only six feet high; *Hipparion*, the little three-toed horse; the huge pig *Stylochoerus*, three feet high at the shoulder with tusks almost a yard long, trotting through the grass; *Pelorovis oldowayensis*, a giant water buffalo with horns six feet across; and of course the familiar animals— ostriches, zebras, antelopes, hippos. And overhead, endless flocks of birds: ducks, crows, thrushes, geese, storks, herons and in the distance some buzzards circling over the dead and the dying. The savannah was the animals' sea, and they moved in it like fish.

We walked slowly on, looking around all the time, still sensing invisible eyes watching us. Even Nuell got the idea. He stopped every few minutes and gazed around him, trying to see movement in the tall grass. We covered a mile and then another mile. The sun, K27, was past the zenith and heading down the far side of the sky toward the horizon. But because the Pleisto day was so long, it would still be several hours before it set. That was good and bad—good, because it gave us time to track the hominids who were holding Professor Joher captive; bad, because it mean we still had a lot of heat to endure. The sun had been baking the plain for twelve hours. Heat shimmered in waves from the grass. We were sweating a lot and beginning to gasp for breath. We could easily become dehydrated if we didn't find water soon.

The ground was rising now. We were going up one of the low, rolling hills that rose out of the plain. It was hard work. Our mouths were dry and we were beginning to feel tired. We hadn't eaten anything for several hours. "It'll be easier going down the other side," Weddy said.

And then from the distance came a shrill cry, like a nail driven across glass. It chilled us and we stopped dead in our tracks. The sound hung in the air like a thin line, not human, not animal, high and sharp. Right after it came a chorus of snarling and barking.

"It might be Dad," Nuell cried. "Let's go."

We charged up the hill, panting and soaked with sweat. Suddenly, I was afraid that Nuell might just charge down the other side into whatever was down there. As we came to the crest I called in a hard whisper, "Everybody down." We dropped flat and stared out from the hilltop.

It was more of the same landscape, but set into it was a huge lake which went on as far as we could see, until it disappeared in the haze. Along its edge was a fairly wide pebbly beach, and in the water beyond the beach, patches of swampy papyrus reeds. There were acacia woods here and there along the shore. Out in the water, in the open places among the reeds, stood pelicans and great pink flamingos, feeding at the end of day. In the middle of the lake were several small islands.

But we hardly saw any of this, because there was something else down there that gripped us much more. Straight ahead on the beach, about a half mile away, were a dozen or so creatures, about three feet tall. They stood in a kind of half-crouch, sometimes rising straight up, sometimes resting their weight on their knuckles, as gorillas do. They faced the lake, barking and snarling at a larger creature they'd cornered against the reedy swamp. Every few seconds, two or three of them would dart out toward the big one, trying to get in a hit with their fists, or a quick rip with their teeth. They walked with a kind of waddle, but it was surprising how fast they could move.

The biggest one was about five feet tall. He was holding in both hands a club of some kind—probably a piece of tree branch, although we couldn't tell exactly at our distance. We couldn't make out his face, either, but clearly he was in trouble, because the little ones were getting in some good blows and he was backing deeper into the water. I felt sorry for him; there'd be crocodiles in that lake.

One thing about him was clear, though: Whatever his size and shape, he was a human being.

3.

We lay at the top of the hill, gasping in the baking sun, but glad to rest. I was feeling all sorts of queer things. We were seeing something that no human being had ever seen—our own ancestors as living beings instead of as a bunch of fossilized bones, the way I'd always seen them before. I felt awed and filled with a kind of crazy excitement. I guess it would be like seeing God for some people. I'd spent years thinking about ancient humans, studying them and even dreaming about them at night. I'd make up daydreams, too, of seeing one of them in the flesh—going to this obscure swampy area in East Africa and finding a tribe of them hiding away from modern people. But I'd always known those were daydreams. Yet here I was, staring down a hillside at the creatures who'd filled my life for years, and inside I was dancing with the excitement of it.

"What are they, Char?" Weddy whispered, sort of awed herself.

"They're human beings, Weddy. They're human beings, and we're the first modern humans ever to see any."

"No," Nuell said.

"What?"

"Dad. He saw them this morning."

I hadn't thought of that. "But still," I said.

"Who are they then, Char?" Weddy asked.

I thought quickly. In Pleistocene times on earth several types of hominids all existed at once. Actually, scientists disagreed as to how they should be categorized. Some lumped a lot of individual fossils into one species, others made separate species out of them. According to Professor Joher, you had *Australopithecus africanus*, who was around four and a half feet high; *Australopithecus robustus*, who was the same sort of hominid, but bigger boned; and *Homo habilis*, generally considered a true human being. The australopithecines made tools—at least *africanus* did—but we weren't sure whether he hunted or not. *Homo habilis* was more advanced. He made a lot of different kinds of tools of stone and probably bone and wood, too. He constructed rough windbreak shelters and he definitely hunted. Besides these hominids, there were also a variety of more apelike types in between the hominids and the true apes.

Today we have only one hominid, man, and three great apes—chimpanzees, gorillas and orangutans. But back then there were more—a whole spectrum of large primates ranging from true human types through ape-men, to true apes.

"I'll tell you what I think," I said finally. "I think the big one is a *Homo habilis*. He's using a club and I don't think the australopithecines could do that. I think the little ones are ramapithecines—sort of semi-apes, semi-men."

Down on the beach the barking and snarling was increasing. The *Homo habilis*—if that's what he was—was now up to his waist in the water, his club poised overhead. He moved awkwardly, as if he were limping on one foot. "Let's rescue him," Nuell said suddenly.

It was a tempting idea to me. I wanted to see him close up, to touch him, to talk to him even.

"I don't think we should," Weddy said. "We're not supposed to interfere with the fauna."

"I still think we should," Nuell said.

"Why?" I demanded. I was hoping he'd have a good excuse.

"Because he knows where Dad is."

Weddy and I turned our heads to look at Nuell. I knew him well enough to keep my mouth shut when he said something crazy until I heard his reasoning. "How do you figure, Nuell?" I said.

"He's got to be one of the ones who jumped Dad this morning. You can see he's hurt. There's something wrong with one of his legs. I figure maybe Dad hurt him somehow when they jumped him. Then when the others went off with Dad, he couldn't keep up because of his leg and these little guys jumped him."

"That's pretty speculative, Nuell," I said.

"Nuell," Weddy said, "even if he knows where Dad is, how would we get him to lead us there? He probably can't talk."

"I don't know," Nuell said. "We could figure something out."

"He might have some kind of rudimentary speech," I said. "It wouldn't be very good, but it might be something."

"Come on, I feel like doing it," Nuell said.

"So do I," I said. "It's worth taking the chance."

"We have to make up our minds fast," Nuell said. "They're going to get him pretty soon."

Nuell was right. The hominid—whatever type he was—was still backing into the water. He had the club over his head, and when the little ones dashed out at him he'd take a swing at them. But he was tired, I could see that, and they were coming at him in two's and three's. His shoulders were drooping and once his head went down. I could tell how he felt—desperate and scared and exhausted and not sure how to save himself. I felt sorry for him. I'd been that way myself a lot when I was a little boy—not attacked like that, but all alone and scared and not knowing what to do. "Let's do it," I said.

We looked at Weddy and she looked into our faces. "We're not supposed to," she said.

"But if he knows where Dad is?"

"Yes," she said. "All right."

Suddenly, the hominid made a dash for the shore, swinging his club wildly over his head and splashing water up around. The little ones curled around him, attempting to hit at him and then ducking away from the club. When he hit the shore he turned and started to run along the beach. With his longer legs and upright stance he could easily have outdistanced them. But he was limping and he could not escape, and the little ones pounded at him from all sides and ducked away. Then one of them leaped onto his back. He reached around behind him to grab at the attacker, but then another one leapt on, and another. He stumbled, staggered forward under the weight and fell. In an instant, the smaller creatures, barking and howling, piled on him.

And the same moment we were up and charging down the hillside, shouting, holding out the electro-prods. At our shouts, down on the pebbly beach the little creatures froze. A flock of pelicans rose heavily into the air with a thick, flapping noise. We charged on, the shiny aluminum rods of our prods stuck out before us like swords. The little primates had climbed off the big one and were now standing in a group staring up at us, making low, guttural noises. We charged on in a line. At twenty yards we pulled up.

We could see them clearly now and could smell a

soft, musty animal smell. They stood with fists upraised, growling loudly. Their shoulders were stooped, their knees bent, their feet splayed outward. They were covered with a light growth of reddish hair. Their heads were flat and their mouths and jaws extended out of their faces in short muzzles. Their arms were long in proportion to their bodies, and their thumbs appeared to be twisted out of place, so that they lay alongside their fingers instead of opposing them. There was something doglike about them, something apelike, something human. It gave me a queer feeling to look at them—they were so familiar and at the same time so strange. Across two million years of evolution we gazed at them, and waving their fists, they snarled back.

The bigger one had been lying face down, but now he rolled over on his back. Two or three of the little creatures near him snarled.

"Hey," Nuell shouted.

The little ones turned toward us again and went on snarling. "Hold it, Nuell," I said. "Let's see what they do."

Suddenly, the wounded one sat up and blinked around at us, looking confused and scared. He reached out an arm, fumbling in the pebbly sand for his club. Instantly, three of the little ones jumped on him and slammed him flat into the sand.

"Hey," Nuell shouted. He dashed forward, the electro-prod extended, and flipped it like a sword across the shoulders of the three little ones. They shrieked and rolled off the big one. They'd never felt an electric shock before and it scared them. For a minute they sat in the sand sort of gibbering and looking nervously at Nuell. Slowly, Nuell stepped forward with the prod out in front of him. The three little hominids jumped up and dashed back into the group where they'd be safe. They all began gibbering at Nuell and shaking their fists at him.

But attacking them with the prods worried me. We weren't supposed to do it. We weren't supposed to mess up the ecological system of Pleisto any more than we could help. If we started chasing these little ones around we could end up hurting them or injuring a pregnant mother or scaring them out of their natural habitat. Besides, I'll admit, I wasn't as aggressive as Nuell. I didn't like hurting things. "Let's go easy, Nuell. Maybe we can scare them off some other way."

"How?"

"By shouting," Weddy said.

"It won't work," Nuell said.

"Let's try," I said. I began to wave my arms and shout, feeling sort of foolish. Weddy shouted, too, and Nuell tipped his head back and let out some yips. All that happened was that the little hominids barked louder and shook their fists more vehemently. "I told you it wouldn't work," Nuell said.

I shrugged. We didn't have much choice. "Okay," I said. "But let's try not to hurt them." I stuck out my prod, and so did Nuell and Weddy. We lunged together like swordsmen, sort of slapping at the little creatures.

They began to shriek and mill around, looking confused. They pulled back. We moved forward. They pulled again and then they broke and ran in that waddle. We chased after them a short distance down the beach until they swerved into a patch of acacia that bordered the lake. In a minute they had disappeared into the dappled sunshine of the woods. We stopped and turned back.

The wounded hominid was up on his feet. He'd gotten hold of his club and when he saw us looking at him he began to limp off as fast as he could in the other direction. Instantly, Nuell flung down his prod and darted after him. The hominid tried to hobble faster, but Nuell was taller and faster anyway, and he closed in quickly. The hominid turned and raised his club. Nuell kept pouring on. Then, ten feet from the creature, he gave him a head fake. The hominid swung the club, aiming for Nuell's head. Nuell dove under the swing and tackled the hominid, who hit down hard on the pebbly beach, grunting. Then Nuell was sitting on his chest.

Weddy and I came up. "Did you see that beautiful head fake, you guys?" he said.

Weddy shook her head. "You'll never change, Nuell."

Now, finally, we had a chance to examine the hominid close up. He was a little under five feet, as close as I could judge. He had a coat of hair, like the other ones, but finer and lighter, about as thick as what you'd find on a really hairy modern human. But the rest of his body, leaving aside his head, wasn't much different from ours. His feet were somewhat splayed out and he seemed a bit heavier and rougher for his size.

It was his head that made the difference. He didn't have much of a forehead—it was only a couple of inches from his eyebrows to his hairline. His skull was pretty flat and his eyes were set back under a ridge that looked like great eyebrows. His nose was flat and his chin didn't jut out like a modern human's, but receded back so that his thin lips and mouth were thrust forward in a short muzzle. Staring at him, I got that curious feeling again, as if somehow I were looking at a strange twin of myself—somebody who was me and wasn't me at the same time.

"What do you think, Char?" Weddy said.

"I'm pretty sure he's *Homo habilis*," I said. "It means 'the handy man.' They call him that because he could make things." I paused. "He's a human being, all right."

The hominid lay on the ground as we stood over him, staring, and suddenly I felt pity for him. He was helpless and I knew he was scared half to death at seeing people like us. We must have looked weird to him, with our swollen heads and clothes and hairless skin, like visitors from Mars in an old science fiction story. The poor creature, I thought—alone and friendless among strangers.

The creature shifted the position of his leg on the sand and Weddy pointed. "Look," she said. "That's the trouble. He's bleeding from the side of his foot."

We bent. It was true: He'd been gashed somehow just around the side of the arch. Weddy stooped. "I'm going to have a look at it." Nuell squatted by his head to keep him quiet, and Weddy dabbed at the wound with her handkerchief. It was filled with dirt.

"That must hurt, that dirt. Let's carry him down to the lake so I can wash it out," Weddy said.

Nuell lifted him by the shoulders and I took the feet. He struggled for a minute and then he gave up and went limp, resigned to his fate. We carried him to the edge of the lake and laid him there with his feet in the water so Weddy could wash the wound. She dabbed it. "It's a pretty clean cut," she said.

"I told you so," Nuell said.

I looked at him. "You told us what?"

"That he knew where Dad was."

Weddy and I looked at him, puzzled.

"Sure," he said. "Don't you see? Where could he get a clean cut like that."

Then it dawned on me. "You're right, Nuell."

"Sure I'm right. The only thing on this planet that could have given him a clean cut like that is Dad's specimen knife."

4.

The trouble with me was I liked Weddy too much and I didn't think she liked me. Oh, she liked me, but not the way I liked her. She was so pretty, with her light brown hair and brown eyes that sparkled when she laughed. She was never mean; she was always fair. When Nuell and I got into an argument, which we did a lot, she would try to see both sides of it and settle it.

The thing was, I think she liked Nuell better. Nuell was her younger brother. Weddy was my age, Nuell was a year younger than us. That was why she liked Nuell better than me: He was her brother, he'd known her all his life and she'd only known me for five years.

Anyway, I figured she didn't think I was good enough for her. Who was I? My father left when I was three or four. I hardly knew him. I can remember a big man with a mustache, sitting on his lap while he jounced me up and down saying, "Ride a cock horse," and wishing he wouldn't do it because he was jouncing me too hard. That's about all I remember.

I don't know whether his leaving made my mother get the way she was, or if he left because she got that way, but anyway, a lot of the time she wasn't able to do very much. She'd tell me she was having one of her bad times and get me to go to the drugstore for her pills, and then she'd get into bed and stay there for days, or even a couple of weeks. And I'd have to take care of things—clean the house and shop and cook her dinner, besides going to school, of course. When I was little, Granny Slyte used to come in and help when my mother had one of her bad times, but Granny Slyte was getting old and couldn't do it any more. So I had to do it. Even when my mother was better she didn't do much. She didn't clean the apartment and she cooked mostly de-hydrated stuff you could just throw in a pot with some water.

That was the reason why I did so well at school. I hated going home to that messy old apartment, so in the afternoons I'd go to the science lab and work on something, or sit in the public library and read. I got so far ahead of my class that they had to let me take ad-vanced courses. This was when I was around nine or ten. Then, when Professor Joher came around looking for a kid to come in afternoons to sweep his laboratory and clean things up, they thought of me, because I was the only kid in my class who knew about lab equipment. Besides, they knew I needed to make a little money.

When it happened I couldn't believe it. I'd heard of Professor Joher, of course. He was the most famous man around the town. The first time I went to his lab I was so scared I could hardly sweep—scared that I'd break something or do something wrong and get fired. But I didn't, and after a while I got used to it. Of course, I got curious about the stuff he had around the laboratory—fossil bones, stone tools, soil samples, bits of rock with marks in them of pollen from flowers that had died a million years ago. I began to read up on it—on the history of human evolution, on the methods of archeology, on the flora and fauna of ancient times, on how early man lived, hunted, worked. And sometimes when I was alone in the lab, I'd open drawers and look at the things stored there, trying to teach myself to identify the bones and stones. I never touched anything; I just looked. But anyway, I was pretty worried that if Professor Joher caught me he'd fire me.

Then one day he did catch me. I was looking at an array of ancient teeth in a drawer. I was so engrossed in trying to identify them all that I didn't hear Professor Joher come in. Suddenly, he was standing behind me.

"What are you doing, Char?" he snapped.

I swiveled around, scared. "I didn't touch anything, sir," I said quickly. "I swear, I was just looking."

"Looking? For what?"

I began to go hot and red. I could feel the sweat begin to run down the side of my face. "I was trying to guess what they were."

"You were identifying the fossils?"

"I was trying, sir." I wiped my face with my sleeve, praying that somehow I could make him understand so he wouldn't fire me. "I'm interested in it."

He stared at me for a moment. Then he reached into the drawer and pulled out a tooth. "What's this?" he said.

I looked at it. It was pretty easy. "It's an australopithecine molar—I think."

He took out another tooth. "And this?"

"Dryopithecine cheek tooth."

Swiftly, he pulled open another drawer and took out a bone. "And this?"

I looked at it carefully. "Femur, sir," I said.

"Of what?"

I looked at it again. I was sort of puzzled. It seemed like a trick question. But I took a chance. "Modern man, sir?"

He dropped the bone back into the drawer. "Extraordinary," he said. "How did you come to know all this?"

"I've been reading up, sir."

He laughed and finally my heart stopped pounding. "I guess you have," he said. He took me into his office and gave me a cup of tea and asked me a lot of questions—about myself and my family and school, and what I wanted to do with my life and so forth. And the next day he went around to my school and said he was taking me on as a student assistant; I needn't go to school any more. I was twelve years old. That was the day I learned what joy felt like.

At first I went home every night the way I'd been doing. But sometimes I'd have to stay late to finish up something I was working on and I'd spend the night in the lab on a cot. After a while it got so I was spending most of my nights there. Finally, Professor Joher had a little storage room cleaned out for me and I moved in. I began eating dinner with the Johers and I became a member of the family. Sort of. It was kind of a funny way to be. I *wanted* to be part of the family—I wanted that a lot. And sometimes they treated me like I was. But other times I wasn't. For example, on somebody's birthday they'd have a party and I'd be part of it just like the rest of the family. But in the summer, when they went on vacation to Mrs. Joher's father's house in the country, I didn't go. It was just them. They left me to look after things. I knew they felt that I wouldn't expect to go along with them. And I didn't, but the first night after they left I lay in bed and cried.

So you can see why I figured Weddy didn't think I was good enough for her. I wasn't sure that I was, either. I could see that she wouldn't necessarily like me. Who was I? She was the daughter of a famous scientist, and I didn't even know where my father was. But I liked her. I liked her a lot. And I was determined to be a great scientist so she'd come to like me, too.

By the time we got the hominid's foot cleaned and bandaged, the sun had gone down the sky and was hanging over the tree line at the horizon, hot and red. In the opposite direction, across the lake, the light fell pink upon the white volcanic mountains and turned the flamingos red as cooked lobsters. We took off our clothes and cooled ourselves in the lake. Then we sat on the pebbly beach trying to figure out what to do next. The hominid sat a few feet away. We'd wrapped a scrap of cloth from Nuell's shirt around the cut and he kept pulling at it in a puzzled way. He'd never seen cloth before. He couldn't figure out what it was.

"Well," Nuell said, "we got him. The big question is whether he can tell us where Dad is."

"He can't be too far away," Weddy said. "They must have a campsite somewhere around here."

These early hominids, I knew, were nomads. Each little band had a territory it traveled around in, going to places where it knew the berries would be ripe, or there'd be honey or good fishing and hunting spots. It'd camp for a few days at a regular campsite and then travel on. One band would cross and recross the same territory thousands of times for maybe hundreds of years. It'd get to know it the way I knew the inside of my room back in the lab.

"A lot of times they camped in dry riverbeds where they come down to the lake," I said. "The walls of the riverbed would protect them from the wind a little. They liked living by water. They ate a lot of stuff like catfish, frogs, turtles, even water birds."

"That shouldn't be so hard to find," Nuell said. "All we have to do is go around the lake until we come to it."

"No good, Nuell," I said.

"Why not?" he demanded.

"Because we don't know which way around the lake to go. For all we know it could be a hundred miles around. If we start off the wrong way it could take us a couple of weeks to go around."

"All right," he said. "Then what?" He was sore at me for ruining his idea. I looked quickly at Weddy to see if she was sore at me, too.

But she wasn't. "The thing is," she said in her calm, thoughtful way, "the hominid knows where his gang went. He'd know which direction to go in, if we could get him to tell us."

Suddenly, I was excited. "Nobody knows if these hominids have language," I said. "It would be a big breakthrough if we could learn to talk to them."

"We could probably force him to talk," Nuell said. "We're bigger than he is."

"How would you do it, Nuell?" I asked. I didn't think it was likely to work.

"No," Weddy said softly. "No forcing. He's a human being like us."

Nuell gave Weddy his grumpy look, but he didn't say anything. I said, "We're pretty sure that these hominids have some system of communication. They live in groups and work in groups and hunt in groups. They had to be able to signal each other when there were animals near, or enemies around, or shout out orders or something. But we don't know if they have an actual language or just used gestures and sounds for signals."

Nuell stood up. "I'm going to try to talk to him," he said. He walked over to where the hominid sat moodily in the sand. When he saw Nuell come toward him he followed him warily with his eyes. Nuell crouched down in front of him. "Okay, Handy man," he said. Then he pointed to the piece of bandage on his foot and made a slashing gesture with his hand.

The hominid made a low, throaty growl and pulled himself back. Now Nuell pointed to himself and pantomimed the slash again. The hominid growled and rose up on his knees, ready to run or fight if he had to.

"You're just scaring him," Weddy said.

"Yes, don't scare him, Nuell."

Nuell looked around at us. "All right, you try it," he said.

I looked at Weddy. She reached down inside her shirt and pulled out the locket she always wore. It was a little gold oval and inside it were pictures of her father and her mother. She opened the locket, slipped out the picture of her father, closed the locket and put it back down inside her shirt. Then she went over to the hominid, crouched down in front of him and held out the little picture. "Do you recognize this, Handy?" she said.

For a moment he stared at it, puzzled, but curious. He'd never seen a picture of anything before. Then suddenly, before Weddy could move, he slashed out with his palm and banged the picture out of Weddy's hand. "Ka," he snapped out.

"Hey," Nuell cried and we both jumped to our feet. Handy was sitting back, growling, his eyes narrowed, his lips curled away from his teeth. Quickly, Weddy snatched the picture up from the ground and moved back again.

"Ka," the hominid growled again. "Ka."

A chill ran up my spine. "Do you know what?" I cried. "He's talking. He's talking to us."

But I didn't get a chance to say anything more, for at that moment there rose into the brown dusk air a shrill, knife-edged shriek, followed by a lot of barks and growls. The shriek went on and on, hanging in the air like a great scimitar, stopped abruptly, started again and then shut off in a quick squeal.

5.

We stood there, shaken, in the deadly silence that remained after the shriek was cut off. Handy was up on his knees, tense and alert. We waited, but there was nothing more. "Somebody's got something," Nuell said finally.

"A big cat," Weddy said. "Maybe a saber-tooth."

I realized now that we were in trouble. Camping out on the savannah we were certain to be spotted by some predator. We were being noisy and careless and we'd left an obvious trail across the plains. Out there in the gathering darkness were a lot of animals looking for a meal—lions and saber-tooths and snakes and even predatory birds. I'd been stupid. We never should have stayed out in the savannah. We should have headed back for the spaceship before dark. I'd gotten so excited about finding the hominid I hadn't thought about the coming of night. But it was too late for that now; crossing the savannah in the dark was certain to bring the cats down on us. "Listen," I said, "we've got to find a safe place to spend the night. We should have thought of it before."

Suddenly I felt angry. Why was it my fault that we hadn't thought of it? Why was I always the one who was supposed to see that everything worked okay? "Listen," I said, looking at them. "It isn't my fault."

Weddy stared at me. Then in her quiet voice she said, "Why do you always think everything is your fault, Char?"

I blushed. Why did I? "Somebody has to be in charge," I said.

Weddy went on staring at me. "Why do they?"

I went on blushing. "Things don't get done if nobody's in charge."

"Yeah, but why is it always you?" Nuell said.

"Nuell, butt out," Weddy said sharply. "Don't start another argument."

"Me?" he said. "You started the whole thing."

Somebody did have to be in charge, I thought. "Okay, let's all shut up for a minute," I said.

Nuell swung back to me. "Listen, Char—"

"Char's right, Nuell," Weddy said. "Let's be quiet for a minute. It's my fault. I started the whole thing."

So we stood there not saying anything, and not looking at each other either, trying to calm ourselves down. Finally, Nuell said, "Okay, now what?"

Weddy gestured at Handy. "Where do they go at night?"

"There'd be a lot of them—the whole band," I said. "They'd probably post guards. It'd be too many for an animal to attack."

They were silent. "What are we going to do then?" Weddy asked.

"We could ask him where to go," Nuell said, jerking his head toward the hominid.

It was a good idea—if we could figure out a way to do it. I crouched down on my haunches, frowning, and thought about it for a minute. Weddy and Nuell sat down in the sand. When I'd got it thought through, I said, "I'm pretty sure he's got some kind of language. That wasn't just a sound he made when Weddy showed him the picture of your dad. That was a word. 'Hate' or 'kill' or something like that. Something with anger in it."

"He's sure sore at Dad, whatever it was," Nuell said.

"I think he's more scared than anything," Weddy said. "He's probably never seen anything as sharp as that specimen knife. It would have been like magic to him. He's bound to be frightened of us. I mean, we must look pretty funny to him."

"This isn't getting us any place to sleep," Nuell said. "I think we should just go out and look around."

"Let's try out Handy first," I said. "He must know

some safe place to go—a cave or the ledge of a cliff or something. These guys would know this territory like the back of their hands." But it wasn't just a sleeping place I wanted. I was curious as I could be to try to talk to the hominid. It would be the most fantastic scientific triumph if I could.

"I agree with Char," Weddy said.

Whenever she said something like that, I got a thrill up my back. It was silly, but I wanted her to like me and I couldn't help it. Suddenly, I wanted to give her something. "You try, Weddy," I said, filled with generosity.

Her brown eyes met mine. "I don't know if I can," she said.

"Try," I said. "He might be less afraid of a female than a male."

"Do you think he knows that I'm a girl?"

It was a funny question, and in the dark I blushed. She had breasts—surely Handy could see that. "I think he must," I said.

"I don't know," she said. "Our clothes might fool him. We all probably look pretty much the same to him."

She was right, I realized. "Try anyway," I said.

Handy was still poised in a crouch, tense and ready to run. Weddy rose, walked over to him and knelt in front of him, so that her face was level with his. Then she placed her palms together and laid her cheek against them, her head tipped, her eyes closed. "Sleep," she said. "Sleep."

The hominid stared at her, frowning, puzzled. "He doesn't get it," Nuell said.

But I didn't want Weddy to feel discouraged. "We don't know for sure what he's thinking," I said.

Weddy opened her eyes and looked at Handy. Then she lay down in the sand, curled up into herself, again with her eyes closed and her hands against her cheek. "Sleep," she said. "Sleep, sleep."

Handy gazed at her for a moment. Then he sat, looked down at his foot and tugged at the bandage, ignoring Weddy. She looked at him and sat up. "Nuell's right. He isn't getting it."

I was disappointed. He had a language—I was sure of that—so he must have some idea of what words were, what "meaning" meant. But he might not understand that his wasn't the only language—that we had one of our own.

"Maybe he just thought she was lying down to sleep," Nuell said. "He probably didn't get that she was demonstrating a word."

"I think that's right," I said. "Maybe it would be better to try to learn his language instead of teaching him ours."

But before I had finished saying it, Handy had leapt to his feet and tense, his arms cocked in front of him, was staring into the tall grass at the edge of the beach. "Bek," he shouted. "Bek."

We looked. Standing there in the deepening dusk, its forepaws in the sandy edge of the beach, stood a smilodon, the great saber-toothed tiger, four feet tall at the shoulder, its eight-inch fangs curving from its upper jaw. Its eyes gleamed in the last faint light of the day, and as we looked its great mouth spread wide in a yawn until the jaws were at right angles to each other, exposing a mass of enormous, wet, yellow, razor-sharp teeth.

We froze. The smilodon closed its jaws and looked us over. "Nobody move," I hissed. The smilodon let out a soft, low growl and stepped out of the tall grass onto the beach. It was now only thirty feet away, its tail twitching, watching, waiting. Out of the corner of my eye I saw Handy, his arms still cocked in front of him, his knees bent. "Handy's going to make a break for it in a minute," I said. "The saber-tooth will jump when he does. Get your prods out, but move easy. Once Handy breaks it's all going to happen fast."

Slowly, I moved my arm around to my side and grasped the base of the electric prod, never taking my eyes off the smilodon. It seemed enormous, big as an elephant, looming there in the dusk, getting ready to jump. I could feel my heart thumping in my chest. My mouth was dry and my hands were cold and wet.

The smilodon moved its head a little and then back again, looking from one of us to the next, trying to decide which one of us to go for. Suppose it was Weddy? Suppose he leaped and she fell and he snapped that massive jaw around her face? "Weddy," I said softly, "try to stay with Handy when he runs. Go after him."

Out of the corner of my eye I saw her nod. Once

again the smilodon yawned, exposing those giant fangs, long and sharp as butcher knives. Its mouth closed. Its tail dropped. Its legs collapsed under it and it crouched. Handy broke and ran up the beach. Fear whistled through me like a cold wind. I snapped the rod of the prod out, and at the same moment the smilodon seemed to rise into the air and float there, diving for Weddy, an enormous gray blur in the twilight. Nuell and I jumped apart, and as it sailed past us, we jabbed hard with the prods. When the prods hit, the smilodon seemed to bunch together in midair, its head pulling into its shoulders, its legs jerking up against its chest. Its poise was broken, and it dropped awkwardly to the sand short of the two figures racing up the beach along the water's edge. For a couple of seconds it sprawled there, and then it heaved itself up and shook itself.

"Let's go," Nuell shouted. He rushed for the animal, and I went with him, scared to death and wondering how Nuell could be so brave. "Take one side," he shouted, "and I'll take the other." We jutted our prods forward. It turned to face us, its back now to the water, dark and still, and I could smell the musky animal smell. As it faced the fading twilight, its eyes were like huge yellow marbles, and it roared, making a snatching gesture with its fangs. I lunged forward with the prod. The animal snapped out a paw the size of a baseball glove to bang at the prod. I pulled it back, and at the same time, Nuell hit it from the other side. Now the smilodon swung its mammoth head around toward him.

Its mouth gaped wide and it roared, and I jabbed again from the blind side. It shuddered, trying to shake off the shock, and swung its head toward me, confused and blinking. I threatened with the prod, and now Nuell hit it from his side. The smilodon stepped backward, snarling and snapping its great jaws so hard I could hear the teeth click. It seemed unbelievable to me that we were standing so close to this enormous animal, close enough to smell the mustiness, see its mustache twitching, hear the teeth clicking. My hands were shaking. It turned its huge eyes on me and opened its jaw. I could almost have reached my hands into its mouth. "Jab him, Nuell," I shouted.

Nuell jabbed. The smilodon swung its head back and I jabbed. The smilodon stepped backward. We moved forward, keeping pace and jabbed again. It stepped backward once again, and we darted forward, like fencers, jabbing and jumping back again. The animal was confused and unhappy with the shocks hitting it over and over. It couldn't figure out what to do, and it kept on backing away, snapping and snarling and slapping out with those great paws at the prods. We stayed with it and in a moment more it suddenly gave up, turned and loped off across the sand into the dusk and the tall grass.

Without thinking what I was doing, I threw my arm over Nuell's shoulder and kind of squeezed him. "Yahoo," he shouted, and he threw his arm over my shoulder, too. We stood there for a moment, grinning at each other.

For the first time ever, I felt what it must be like to have a brother. Then we began to feel sort of embarrassed, and we took our arms down and stood facing each other.

"Were you scared, Nuell?"

"Are you kidding?" he said. "I sure was."

"Boy, I was," I said. "My hands were shaking so hard I could hardly hold the prod." It was funny, I thought. We were always fighting with each other, and yet we could be good friends. I wondered if we would stay that way.

"But all the same," he said, "it was a great feeling to be right up close to him like that. He was beautiful."

I shook my head. "You can have it, Nuell." I turned and looked up the beach. Weddy and Handy were a good quarter of a mile up the beach, almost invisible in the dusk. "Let's go," I said. We kept our prods unlimbered in case the smilodon should decide to come back for another try, and jogged after them. With his bad leg Handy could not make much time, and we caught up with them in less than five minutes.

"Hey, Weddy," Nuell called.

She turned to look and I said, "Don't stop Handy. Let's see where he takes us."

"Maybe he isn't going any place," Nuell said. "Maybe he's just running away."

In the dark I gazed at him. Why were we always arguing with each other? "He knows this territory. He'd be bound to run for safety."

At the sound of our voices the hominid turned his

head to look at us over his shoulder. He slowed his pace a little, but then when he saw that we weren't trying to stop him, he turned away again and went on loping along with his limp.

It was quite dark now and we could only see a little way out into the lake. Up ahead the beach curved into the lake so that a patch of forest loomed in front of us. Handy went on running up the beach, following the curve. The beach narrowed, until it was only a thin track at the base of a small bluff that dropped down from the tree line to the water. Handy slowed down and then he stopped. Warily, he looked back over his shoulder at us.

Ahead the forest ended, and land dipped down under the water in a stretch of papyrus reeds. Farther out the land rose again, making a small island covered with acacia forest. It was about a hundred yards from shore, and I knew right away that the hominid tribe used the island as a place that was safe from big cats. They could swim, the cats, if they had to, but they wouldn't want to very much.

Handy was still staring at us. I couldn't see his eyes, just two black pools under the overhanging brow. Was he scared of us? Was he grateful that we'd saved him from the smilodon? Did he trust us? Or was he not even human enough to feel things like trust and friendliness? Was he just an instinctive machine like the smilodon, programmed to hunt, mate, sleep and eat?

I didn't want to believe that. I wanted to believe that he was human like me, that he could feel things the way I did. I wanted him to be my friend. I put out my hand to the others. "Hold up," I said. "Don't scare him off." I stepped slowly forward while the others waited and watched. Handy was turned around now, facing me. He went on looking, but he didn't move. I came on until I was close enough to touch him. He still didn't move, but went on watching warily. What was going on in his head? Did he want to be friends, too? Or was he just scared? Slowly, I stretched my arm out, and then I touched his arm. He flinched and blinked, but he didn't move. For a minute we stood there like that, silent. My heart began to beat fast, and I felt awed and sort of scared.

Then suddenly he pulled his arm away from my hand and turned back toward the lake. Weddy and Nuell came up. "He seems a little tamer," Nuell said.

But I didn't want to think of him as a wild animal. "Friendly," I said. "More friendly."

6.

Handy now stepped into the shallow, swampy piece of the lake. There was a path through the reeds, just wide enough for a human being, which ran out toward the island. I figured over the years it had been trampled out by people going back and forth. Handy turned back to us. "Bek," he said and sliced the air with the flat of his hand, palm down. Then he began to slog through the reeds toward the island.

We stepped into the water after him, going in single file. "Bek," Handy said, this time without looking around.

"There's that word again," Weddy said. "It was what he said when he saw the smilodon."

"I'll tell you what I think," Nuell said. "I think it

means 'danger' or 'look out' or something like that. He's warning us about crocodiles."

"Yes," I said. I didn't want Nuell to get in there with everything first. "It figures that they would have a limited vocabulary with one word standing for a lot of things. You know how a little kid who's just learning to talk will learn a word like 'broke' and use it for a whole lot of things—a dent on a car or a dead bug or a worn-out shoe. I think these early hominids worked the same way. They'd have a word for 'tree' first, and then they'd develop words for different types of trees later."

"What I think," Nuell said, "is that we ought to shut up and watch out for crocs."

He was sore that I had got it over him on the language thing, but he was right and we shut up and slogged on behind Handy toward the safety of the island. But I was excited. We were the first people to have communicated with a member of another human species. You couldn't say that we'd had a conversation with Handy yet, but he'd told us something, and we'd understood.

But I couldn't think about it any more. The water was nearly up to our waists. I knew about Pleistocene crocodiles: They were huge, with heads a yard long and teeth that could shear off a leg the way I'd bite off a carrot, and I kept swinging my head from side to side looking for signs of movement on the dark surface of the lake.

"These guys aren't stupid," Nuell said suddenly. "They left most of the reeds standing. Any croc that came through them would rustle them around pretty good." We plowed on, and after a bit the bottom began to rise. On the island ahead we could now make out individual trees on the low bank above the water. In a minute we were there and climbing up after Handy onto the bank.

Again he stopped and I saw the reason why. Running along the top of the bank as far as we could see in the dark was a thick hedge of thorny branches torn from acacia trees and heaped together to make a long fence three feet high. For a moment Handy stood there in the dark looking around. Then he moved a few feet along the fence and passed through it. We followed and found a narrow passage through the thorns. We slipped through and in a minute we were in a small clearing in the forest. In the middle of the clearing was a shallow pit, about ten feet in diameter and two feet deep in the center. The bottom was covered with dried leaves and crushed reeds. I figured that the hominid tribe—maybe even tribes from different hominid species—had been using the island as a safe sleeping spot for a long, long time, centuries, or even thousands of years.

"What do you figure they dug it out with, Char?" Nuell said.

It wasn't really like Nuell to ask my opinion about something, and I realized that he was trying to be friendly. I guessed that he'd been thinking some of the same things I'd been thinking—about how friendly we felt after we'd fought off the smilodon, and how we were arguing again five minutes later. "They would have used digging sticks—sharp pointed sticks they could pry the dirt loose with and then throw it out of the hole with their hands." One of the amazing things about human beings is how long they'll keep to a way of doing things once they find one that works. If you study stone tools you see that they go on being the same, without any improvement, for a thousand generations. I figured that however they had dug the sleeping pit, they would have gone on doing it year after year, gradually making it deeper bit by bit.

It was by now completely dark. Pleisto had two moons, and the smaller one was climbing up over the volcanic mountains to the east, looking not much bigger than a yellow rock among the stars in the sky. We were hungry. We hadn't had anything to eat since breakfast that morning with the professor, but with worrying about so many things we hadn't thought much about food. Now that we were a little safer and settling down for the night, we wanted something to eat. But there wasn't much chance of finding anything in the dark, and we just had to forget about it.

The next question was what to do about Handy. I wanted to keep him with us. Partly that was because I was still hoping he'd lead us to Professor Joher. But I wanted to get to know him better, too. I wanted to understand him, I wanted to figure out his language, I wanted to get to be friends with him. "Do you think Handy's likely to run away?" I said.

"I don't see how he can," Weddy said. "It's too dangerous out there."

We decided we ought to stand guard anyway. We drew lots, and Weddy got the first shift. I lay down, and being pretty tired, I fell asleep right away.

Some time later I woke up. I sat up quickly, my heart jumping, and then I realized that Weddy was shaking me by the shoulder. "There's something coming across the water through the reeds toward us," she whispered. By now, the second moon had risen, yellow and larger than the first one, and was tracking after its smaller brother. There was plenty of light to see by. Nuell was already awake and kneeling by the edge of the sleeping pit, his head cocked to catch sounds coming from the water. Handy, too, was up on the rim of the sleeping pit, staring nervously through the dark. He listened. There was a sloshing noise and a low muttering, like a candle in the wind. I picked up my electro-prod and snapped out the rod.

"Bek," Handy said softly, slicing the air with the flat of his hand.

"Bek," I said, and even with my nervousness I was elated to communicate with him.

"Let's go see," Nuell said. We rose up out of the sleeping pit, slipped through the acacia woods as quietly as we could and crouched down behind the wall of thorns. Twin paths of yellow from the moons ran across the lake toward us and disappeared in the reeds. In the moonlight we could see all the way across the papyrus swamp to the shore. Coming along the path through the reeds were a dozen shadowy creatures, wading doggedly through the water and chattering among themselves. They were small, shorter than Handy by six inches at least, and at the deepest places the water came up to their chins. Their foreheads were low, and their faces had muzzles, like dogs. In the moonlight they looked very fragile. They weren't ramapithecines, and they weren't anything like Handy. I knew right away what they had to be, and it excited me. "Australopithecines," I whispered. "Sort of halfway between Handy and the ramapithecines that were attacking him."

"They don't know we're here," Weddy whispered. "It looks like they're coming out to camp for the night."

"They're pretty small," Nuell whispered. "I don't think we'd have any trouble driving them off."

"Why should we do that?" Weddy said. "They have as much right to be here as we do."

That was true, but still, it was hard to know how they'd react when they finally realized that we were there. They might run—they might attack—they might do anything. "Let's be careful," I whispered.

Then Nuell whispered: "Look at Handy."

We looked. Handy was down behind the thorn fence, tense, his short muzzle twitching. In his hand he held a two-foot length of stick he'd picked up somewhere in the forest. He looked less like a human being now and more like a jaguar poised for attack. He made a low animal growl. "There's going to be trouble," Nuell whispered.

"He won't take them on all by himself, will he?" Weddy whispered.

"He thinks we'll go with him," Nuell said.

Suddenly, Weddy rose into a half-crouch, slipped along behind the thorn fence to where Handy was staring tensely out into the reedy water and bent down beside him. She laid a hand on his arm and began to stroke gently. "It's okay, Handy," she said softly.

He swung his head to look at her, and then suddenly he shoved her away from him with such force that she tumbled backward onto the ground. Instantly, Nuell was up. From my crouch I lunged at his legs, knocked him off his feet, and rolled on top of him. "Calm down, Nuell," I hissed.

"Damn it, Char." He struggled under me. "Let me up."

"Calm down," I said. Then I looked at Weddy, who was kneeling up. "Are you okay?" I said in a loud whisper.

"Yes," she said. She began to crawl back toward us.

Now I looked back out into the reedy water. The australopithecines had heard the commotion. They stood stock still in the water, staring intently through the moonlight toward the thorn fence. Undoubtedly, they had been able to see movement behind it. "We have to drive them off," I said. "Let's try shouting."

"It won't work, Char," Nuell said.

"It might."

"It didn't before."

It irritated me to have Nuell argue; we didn't have time for it. The australopithecines were coming toward us again. I could make out their faces clearly in the moonlight now—their doglike muzzles, their low foreheads, their deep-set eyes. They were a complete small band—four males, three females, two with babies in their arms, and two subadults. As they pushed through the water, looking nervously around for crocodiles, they looked small and pathetic, and I knew that we could take them in a fight if we had to. But I didn't want to hurt them.

In a moment they would be at the thorn fence we were hiding behind. I glanced at Handy again. He had risen in a half-crouch, prepared to fight. He was bigger than the australopithecines, and he had the stick: He would be able to do a lot of damage. But I didn't want to see any of them hurt, especially the babies. I stood, tipped my head back and whooped. Handy gave me a puzzled look and I realized that he had expected us to wait in ambush for them. Nuell stood and whooped and then Weddy.

The australopithecines stopped dead, frozen in the moonlight at the water's edge, like statues. We went on whooping. They unfroze and moved, and in a few seconds they were drawn into a tight band, with the four males at the front, the subadults at the rear, and the three women with the babies in the middle. The males in the front bared their teeth, shook their fists and began to snarl like dogs.

"I told you it wouldn't work," Nuell said. "We better charge them with the prods."

He was right. I was disappointed. I looked at Handy. He had risen straight up, with the club gripped high, ready to swing. I didn't think he would charge by himself, but if we went out there he'd sure go with us and he'd be out for blood. "Let's try stones," I said. I stooped and fumbled in the sandy shore. There were plenty of rocks here. With one in each hand I stood. "Try not to hit the babies," I said. I threw, and then Nuell was throwing, too, and Weddy. The australopithecines growled louder and shook their fists, but they were only fifty feet from us and bunched together like that it was hard to miss. They began to ease backward into the reedy water, ducking our stones and looking nervously around for crocodiles. A baby shrieked and began to whimper: We'd hit one of them and it made me wince. "Let's be careful," I said.

We went on throwing and then, as if on some kind of a signal, the whole band turned and began to slog as fast as they could through the reeds back the way they had come. And in the next moment, Handy was up, his club raised high.

"Hey," I shouted. We stood, watching. Handy raced along the fence as fast as he could go on his bad leg, and then charged out into the water, throwing up great splashes with his legs. Then he was on top of the little band of australopithecines. I saw the club rise and flash in the moonlight and flash again.

"No," Weddy shouted. "No, Handy." She was on her feet running along the thicket fence and then through the gap and into the water. Nuell and I raced after her. In the lake Handy's club flashed and flashed and the little band scattered, screeching and chattering. Weddy drove through the water, grabbed Handy around the neck from the rear, and pulled him down on top of her into the water. Handy roared, jerked himself loose and scrambled to his feet, the club rising once again. But then Nuell and I were on top of him.

7.

We took the club away from Handy. Nuell twisted his arm behind his back and pushed him out of the water onto land where he let him go. He glared at us. "Ka," he spat out. "Ka." He went on spitting and growling, but he knew he was beaten. He licked his lips and glanced out into the water. In the bright light from the two moons we could see the little band scrambling out of the water onto the shore. One of them was being supported by two of the others, and another one was holding one arm crooked in front of him and was grasping it with the other hand.

We watched them disappear into the acacia forest on the lake shore. "He did a pretty good job on them," Nuell said.

"He sure did," I said.

"What are we going to do with him?" Nuell said.

"We better take him back to the sleeping pit," Weddy said. "So we can keep an eye on him. He's likely to slip out and go after the little ones again."

Nuell grabbed for Handy's arm again, but Handy jerked back, growling. Nuell raised his prod.

"Don't," Weddy said. "Don't hurt him." So Nuell and I sort of crowded in on Handy and marched him back to the sleeping pit. Nuell lay down to sleep, but I was feeling edgy and I sat on the rim of the pit in the moonlight beside Weddy, tired and nervous and plenty wet. Handy sat on the opposite rim, refusing to look in our direction.

"Why did he do that?" Weddy said softly. She sounded depressed and sad. "There wasn't any need for him to fight. The others were going away."

"He wasn't fighting," I said. "He was hunting."

"Hunting?" She sounded shocked.

"Sure. He was going to kill one of them and eat him."

"Kill one?" She sounded bewildered now. "But are they cannibals, these hominids?"

"Well, no, not really. You can't call it cannibalism. That's eating a member of your own species, and Handy isn't one of them, he's a different species. It would be like a lion eating a jaguar. Or a human being eating a monkey. You and I don't eat monkeys, but over the centuries plenty of human tribes have. The Jivaros in the South American jungle had a staple diet of monkeys."

She was silent, thinking. Then she said, "They do an awful lot of fighting, don't they. First Handy's bunch jumped Dad, and then ramapithecines attacked Handy, and now we've had a battle with these australopithecines. Why can't they all be peaceful with each other?"

I was quiet myself for a bit. Finally, I said, "That's the whole problem, isn't it? Why do human beings back on earth fight all the time?"

"Well, yes," she said. "Human beings are the only species who fight their own kind, aren't they?"

I shook my head. "That's what a lot of people think, but it isn't true. Competition is a basic fact of animal life."

"But I mean war," she said.

I shrugged. "Certain kinds of social insects fight wars. Some of them capture slaves and make them work in their own nests."

"Okay, insects. But not mammals."

I shook my head again. "Chimpanzee groups have been known to fight wars with each other."

She looked at me. "They actually kill each other?"

"Yes. It doesn't happen a lot, but it happens."

"I didn't know that."

"It's the competitive nature of things. Take that smilodon. He sees us as his rightful prey, but so do a lot of the other cats out there. Not to mention snakes and predatory birds and scavengers like jackals and buzzards who eat the remains of somebody else's kill. They're all competing for food and water and everything else."

"But not their own kind," she said.

"No," I said. "That's wrong, too. You take any species that runs in packs or groups, like monkeys or wolves or wild dogs, they're always competing with other groups of their own kind. I mean, if two groups of howler monkeys meet in the forest they'll howl at each other, or make other kinds of threat displays. Most of the time it doesn't come down to actual fighting—they just move out of each other's way. But sometimes these monkey groups will fight each other. It happens more than you think. For some reason neither group will back down and they start to fight. Sometimes they wound each other so badly that some of them die. Or take lions— say a male with a female and cubs. Suppose a more dominant lion comes along and drives off the male and takes the female for his mate. The new one is likely to kill the old one's cubs. It's like he doesn't want to raise somebody else's offspring—he wants to start his own family."

Her head was bowed and she was looking down at her hands, which she was lacing and unlacing. For a long time she didn't say anything, and I just waited. Finally, she said, "What's the use of it, Char? What's the use if everybody's going to fight all the time any- way? Won't there ever be peace?"

She looked at me, and in the moonlight I could see tears shining like silver in the corners of her eyes, then break loose and roll down her cheeks. "Well," I said, "that's why we came here really. That's why the Committee was willing for us to come on out here after the big spaceship broke down. They hoped we would find hominids and study them and find out if they fought, and how they fought, and why they fought. And maybe if we learned enough we might find out why we fight, too."

"We found them," she said bitterly. She wiped her eyes with her hand. "They fight all right. They don't seem to do anything else."

She was silent once more. Then she said, "Anyway, it's all so awful. It's nothing but fighting and murder and war, and they've got Dad, and I'm scared they'll kill him."

I wanted to help her. I felt like putting my arm around her and hugging her and telling her that everything was going to be okay. But I didn't dare do it. Once, a few months before, I'd been sitting in the lab with her, working on a Miocene ape's skull. We were bent over it with our heads sort of together. Dusk had started coming in, but we had been too busy to turn on any lights. I could hear her breathe and I kept thinking about her cheek so close to mine, and after a while I couldn't concentrate on the skull any more; all I could do was think about how much I wanted to kiss her. Finally, I dropped one of the skull pieces. She laughed. "Char, you nut, you can't do anything right today."

We looked at each other in the half-light. I didn't

even think what I was doing. I just leaned forward to kiss her, but she turned her head away and I'd ended up kissing her on the ear. It made me blush and feel foolish and angry with myself. So I wasn't going to try to put my arm around her. But I wanted to. I wanted to touch her, and say that we'd find her father and it would be all right. Instead, I told her I'd stand guard for a while, so she lay down and went to sleep.

The sun came up over the volcanic mountains and shone through the trees, and we sat around on the rim of the sleeping pit, feeling hungry and trying to decide what to do.

"What are we going to do with Handy?" Nuell asked.

"I'm still hoping we can get him to lead us to your father," I said.

"I think we ought to forget that idea," Nuell said.

"I don't think we should," I said. "It might take a little time to get the idea across to him, but in the long run it could be the quickest way. Otherwise, we could go wandering around the plains forever." I knew that wasn't the only reason; partly I wanted to keep Handy because I wanted to see if I could learn his language—Habilese, or whatever you would call it. It would be a terrific scientific achievement. I would be famous. I felt sort of guilty about thinking that way. I mean, it was more important to save Professor Joher than for me to achieve scientific recognition. But still, it might be the best way to save him anyway. "We could try it, at least.

Look, we've already learned two words—'ka,' which means 'anger' or 'kill' or something, and 'bek' which means 'look out.' All we have to do is get a couple of more words like 'find' or 'take.' "

"Forget about it, Char. It'll never work," Nuell said.

Suddenly, Weddy said, "Nuell's right, Char. It might take years to work out something."

"Look, he's bound to be headed for his own band. Your dad has to be with them."

"We don't know that," Weddy said. "For all we know, Dad may be back at the spaceship. He might already have escaped."

I looked at her. I hated arguing with Weddy. "He wouldn't do that, Weddy. If he were with some hominid group, he'd stick with them to study them."

None of us said anything. We waited, and then Weddy said, "No, Char, Nuell's right. We have to forget about Handy."

I knew I had to give in. It was two against one. I felt disappointed about losing my chance to learn Habilese, and hurt that she was taking Nuell's side against me. But it would mess things up if I went on arguing. "Okay," I said. "What do we do with Handy?"

"Just leave him," Nuell said. "Forget about him."

Suddenly, I felt very sad. I remember touching Handy, and his letting me, and how I'd felt he was sort of getting to be my friend. I didn't want to just walk away and leave him like that. I didn't want to leave him all alone in the savannah among those predators.

But I had no choice. "Okay," I said. "Let's go." I got up and walked over to where Handy was sitting on the rim of the sleeping pit. He had been looking at his foot, but when I came over he stopped and looked up at me, wary but not flinching. For a moment we stared at each other. Then I said, "Well, so long, Handy." But he didn't understand me and I just turned away, and we started out through the woods toward the path through the reeds to shore.

As we walked along we decided the best thing to do was to continue on around the lake in the direction we'd been going. Handy had started off that way, which made it a good bet that his people were somewhere along there. The odds were that we'd come on them sooner or later. These bands didn't move continuously, but traveled to a source of food and then camped for a while.

We slipped through the gap in the thorn fence, went down the bank into the water and began to plod through the reeds toward shore. Then, when we were about halfway across, I suddenly heard a splash behind me. A croc, I thought, and my heart jumped. I jerked the electro-prod off my back and swung around.

But it wasn't a crocodile. Instead, it was Handy, shadowing along behind us. "Look," I said. "Handy's coming with us. He's coming with us."

They turned around to look, and as we watched Handy stopped in the water and stared at us warily. "He wants to stick with us for safety," Nuell said.

"He isn't sure we want him to follow us," Weddy said.

I raised my arm and gestured him toward us. "It's okay, Handy," I said. I gestured again. But either he didn't understand, or he didn't trust us, because he went on standing there, watching.

"Let's get out of the water before a croc gets us," Nuell said. "Handy will follow of his own accord."

We waded through the water and onto shore. Then we started along the edge of the lake. Handy limped behind us, staying about thirty feet to the rear—just far enough away from us so he could make a run for it if we came after him. Somehow, I would have to teach him to trust us, so I could get him to teach me Habilese.

But we had another thing to worry about first, which was food. By now we hadn't eaten anything for a day, and sooner or later we'd begin to feel short of energy. As we went along we kept our eyes open for anything to eat. Sometimes we found little patches of berries, but there weren't very many. It seemed likely to me that some group of hominids had taken this route not long before and stripped the area of food. Pretty soon, I realized, we'd have to stop and hunt something, or maybe catch a fish out of the lake. I didn't know how we were going to do that: We didn't know much about hunting, and anyway, we didn't have any weapons but the electro-prods. You couldn't kill anything with them.

There wasn't any shortage of things to hunt, though. In the distance all around us were animals: herds of zebras, giraffes, deinotherium, apes, single hippos or the great pig, stylochoerus; and sunning themselves on rocks were prides of lions or saber-toothed *Megantereon*, or *Pantheras*, a cat something between a lion and a leopard. Then, in the far distance under the baking sun were the snow-capped volcanic mountains, looking cool and inviting. I wished we were up there sucking on some nice, cool snow.

We walked on, feeling hungrier and hungrier, and then at midmorning we came to a campsite. It was down in a dry riverbed, near to where the river widened out to empty into the lake. After a rain it would be full of water, but now it was dead dry. It was about seventy-five feet across at this point, and its walls were almost four feet high. In the middle there was a circular wind-break of thorn branches, about fifteen feet in diameter. They'd made it by jamming the branches into the ground and then propping them up with heaps of stones. Scattered around everywhere were broken bones, some of them old and dry and brown, some of them fresh, with bits of meat still on them. There were skulls, too, mostly broken open to get the brains out. Even standing on the bank of the riverbed I could identify a zebra jaw and the skull of a young *Theropithecus* baboon. Mixed in everywhere were chunks and chips of stones, broken sticks, eggshells, scraps of rotted fish heads and a lot of bird feathers, some of them flamingo pink.

"They sure leave a mess," Nuell said.

"It's a good thing they do," I said. "Most of what

we know about these hominids comes from their garbage piles."

As we stood there, Handy slipped up beside us, looking cautiously at us out of the corners of his eyes. Then, when he saw we weren't going to do anything, he jumped down into the riverbed and began limping around the campsite, snatching up any bits of fresh meat he could find and jamming them into his mouth.

"Somebody's been here just a little while ago," Nuell said.

"Yes," I said. "In this heat that meat would go bad pretty quickly. They must have been here yesterday."

"It's got to be the ones who have Dad," Weddy said.

I didn't know what to think about that. I just wished that everything didn't depend on me so much. Nuell would argue with me, and Weddy would disagree sometimes, too, but when it got down to it, they counted on me to know what to do. It was like being a kid back home with my mother again. I had to look after her, instead of the other way around. But there wasn't anything I could do about it. I had to be in charge whether I wanted to or not, and they wanted me to tell them that their dad had been there and he was okay. "Let's go down and take a look," I said.

We slid down the bank. Handy gave us a look, but when he saw we weren't after him he went on scavenging for meat. I hunkered down and began looking through the debris. Some of the bones were very old.

I guessed that the site had been used for decades, maybe even centuries, although it was hard to be sure, because sometimes these rivers changed their courses, burying old sites. Besides, when the river was running it would wash stuff around: Some of the debris could have come from farther upstream. That was the problem with archeology: If you found the bone of a certain animal in a campsite, you wanted to assume that the hominids there ate that kind of animal. But the bone could have traveled there some other way, maybe hundreds of years after anybody had camped there.

Still, there was a wide variety of bones and a wide variety of stone tools: choppers, made of water-worn cobbles with a rough edge knocked into them; knifelike burins with one sharp edge, probably for scraping; flat stone anvils on which they worked bones and stones; and a lot of sharp chips and flakes which they used for small slicing jobs, like cutting through tendons at joints to butcher an animal into pieces.

Then I looked at the windbreak. There was some debris inside it, but not much; they'd probably done most of their eating and working outside. Anyway, they wouldn't have wanted stones and bones all over the ground where they slept.

There were bits of fur on some of the thorns of the branches, too. They'd flung animal skins over the branches to keep out the weather.

The whole time I'd been looking around, Weddy and Nuell had been watching me. Finally I said, "I'm pretty sure *Homo habilis* used this camp. *Australopithecus* could make stone tools, but not so many different kinds. Besides, I don't think they were smart enough to make a windbreak like that, with skins. The only thing is, a lot of different groups might have used the same campsite. There's no way of knowing for sure who was just here."

"It could have been the ones who have Dad, though, couldn't it?" Weddy's eyes were wide and I could tell that she was almost pleading with me to say yes. I didn't know. I just didn't know. But I judged that it was better not to worry them.

"It could have been," I said, looking at their faces. They still looked troubled. "Probably it was. I think it must have been." But I wasn't anything near that sure.

That was when I noticed that Handy was no longer searching through the rubbish in the camp, but was standing, staring intently up the dry riverbed.

"He heard something," Nuell said.

Handy flapped his hand at us to be quiet. We stood still, watching. Then we heard it, too—a soft whinny, followed by a gentle snort. Instantly, Handy stopped and picked out of the rubble a stone chopper. In another moment a hipparion ambled into sight up the riverbed. When it saw us it stopped and stood staring, its nostrils quivering. I figured it had become separated from its herd and was now wandering around looking for it. It whinnied again.

"Ka," Handy hissed.

It was the word he had used before when he had grown angry at Professor Joher's picture. "That means he wants to kill it," I whispered.

The minute I spoke, Handy snapped his head around and gestured at me with a ferocious wave of his hand. "Tekla," he hissed.

"He wants us to be quiet," Weddy whispered. The new word, I realized, meant something like "don't talk," or "don't move," or maybe just "be still." We stood quiet, watching.

Handy was staring at the hipparion, which was staring nervously back. I figured that it was thirsty and was trying to get to the lake to drink, but it was clearly afraid of us. Now Handy, never taking his eyes from the little horse, slipped cautiously to the edge of the riverbed, climbed the bank and disappeared in the tall grass. "He's trying to get around behind him," Nuell said. "He wants to drive him toward us."

We stood quiet, waiting. I had read about how ancient man must have hunted plenty of times, but now I was seeing it for myself and I was excited. The little horse was looking extremely skittish, constantly turning its head from side to side as if it sensed danger but couldn't figure out where it was coming from. It wanted to get to the water, that was certain. We stood quiet. The little horse whinnied, took a few steps back up the riverbed and whinnied again. "Handy better hurry up," Nuell whispered. "It's about to bolt."

We waited another minute and then, up the riverbed, behind the hipparion, we saw Handy leap out of the grass. The horse heard the sound. It jumped around to face Handy and reared back. Giving a long cry, Handy charged. The hipparion turned to flee down the riverbed toward the lake, but we were blocking its way. We began to shout. The hipparion stopped dead, pivoted and swung around to make a dash up the embankment. It was only halfway up when Handy leaped onto its back and brought the stone chopper down with a loud crack on the hipparion's skull. The little horse screamed and staggered back down the embankment, but it didn't fall. We charged toward it. It reared back, throwing Handy to the ground. Nuell reached it first. He threw himself over its back. Caught off-balance, the little horse flipped sideways. Then Handy was on top of it. As Nuell pinned the animal to the ground, Handy's right hand flashed and flashed again. The horse lay flat, shuddering. Again Handy slashed. The horse lay still.

Handy jumped to his feet, flung his arms into the air and began to leap around the horse shouting, "Maymo, maymo, maymo," at the top of his lungs. Nuell began to dance beside him. "Maymo," he shouted. Then Handy, still dancing from one foot to the other, threw his arms around the three of us, pulling us into a tight bunch. "Gar," he said. "Gar."

I wasn't exactly sure what the word meant, but I knew it was important.

8.

We sat and watched while Handy butchered the little animal with stone tools. It was amazing how quickly he did it. First he skinned it, using the stone chopper to hack a slit in the skin the length of the little horse, and then he cut the skin loose from the flesh with sharp little stone flakes. Once the animal was skinned out he dismembered it joint by joint. Within minutes, he had cut the little horse into a dozen pieces, each of which would make about a meal for one person. It was a technique that had been refined over thousands, maybe millions, of years, and passed down the generations for all that endless amount of time.

Then when he was done, instead of beginning to eat, he did something that surprised us. He took from the pile of meat one of the haunches, probably the most valuable part. Standing, he carried it across to where we were sitting, watching. Then he shoved the haunch toward Weddy. "Riwi," he said. He poked Weddy with the meat. "Riwi."

Weddy looked at me in bewilderment. "What am I supposed to do?"

"Take it," I said. "It's some kind of a gift."

Gingerly, Weddy took the meat. "Now what?"

Handy stood there looking at her. "It's a present," I said. "He wants you to eat it."

"But why me?" she said. "What about you guys?"

"I think he's figured out you're a female," I said. "He's trying to take care of you."

"I can take care of myself," she said. She stood there frowning down at the piece of raw meat she was carefully holding between her fingers.

"Yes," I said, "but if you were a female from Handy's band you wouldn't be able to. You'd be carrying a baby around, or have a little kid tagging after you or be pregnant. You wouldn't be able to join in the hunt without endangering your children. The males would have to bring you food."

"Oh " she said. Handy stood in front of her, staring at her from under those thick eyebrow ridges, and Weddy went on frowning down at the piece of raw meat. "What am I supposed to do?" she said. "I'm not going to eat it raw. I'm not *that* hungry."

"We have to make a fire," Nuell said.

Weddy looked at Handy. Then she set the piece of meat on the ground and patted Handy on the shoulder. "Well thanks, anyway, Handy," she said. "But we have to cook it first."

There were plenty of twigs and broken branches in the campsite. We collected some dried grass and piled twigs on top. Then Nuell removed the plate from the back of his electro-prod, took out the autogenerator, and by holding the two connecting wires a slight distance apart, created a stream of sparks that fell on the dried grass. In a moment it began to smolder.

"Look at Handy," Weddy said. The hominid had stopped eating and was up on his knees, staring intently at the wisps of smoke coming out of the dried grass. Nuell leaned over the fire and blew gently. In a moment, a small flame burst out and a second later Handy was on his feet, dashing back up the dry riverbed.

I jumped up, but I didn't dare chase after him, because I might scare him off. "Handy," I shouted. "Gar, gar."

He was already twenty yards away, but when he heard my voice he stopped and turned around and looked back toward us. I pointed to the fire. "Gar," I shouted. "Gar."

He stood hesitating, not sure what to do. I was sure he'd seen fire often enough, and it had always been dangerous—spurting from a volcanic mountain or racing through the savannah grass of the plain, driving hordes of animals before it. The idea that fire could be a friend—if that was what "gar" meant—was strange to him. He'd never seen a friendly fire before.

But he was curious and he stood watching. The fire was now flaming up nicely, and Nuell was feeding larger branches onto it. I bent over and waved my hand over the flame. "Gar," I shouted.

Handy was now watching intently. "Gar," I called once again. He came a couple of paces forward, walking in a kind of half-crouch, ready to spring back if the fire should suddenly shoot an arm of flame out toward him. I was just guessing, but it seemed to me that to Handy the fire was not just incandescent gases, but a living thing, a dangerous and unpredictable animal that could leap at him if it wanted to.

Once again, I ran my hand swiftly over the flame. "Gar," I said. Handy came closer. "Gar." Then his curiosity overcame his fear, and he skipped quickly up and sat down about ten feet from the fire staring at it intently, still prepared to jump back if the dangerous, uncaged animal should jump at him. Finally, he retrieved his joint of meat and still watching the fire warily, began to gnaw at the bone again.

I was still guessing, but he probably had figured out that just as we were able to drive off the smilodon, so we were able to keep the dangerous animal under control. We were its masters, and it had to obey us. And in a certain way, he was right. It was our fire and we could pretty much make it do what we wanted.

We roasted the meat over the fire and ate it. It

tasted a little bit like beef, but more gamy. The idea of eating horse meat didn't really appeal to any of us very much, but we were hungry and besides, we needed the protein to keep up our strength.

Weddy was looking a lot happier than she had the night before. It was the food, I figured. "You seem more cheerful today, Weddy," I said.

She was sitting cross-legged, gnawing on the bone, a smear of grease around her mouth. "It's like a picnic," she said. "It's nice sitting around together and not fighting for a change. I wish we had some hot dogs instead of this stuff, though."

"It isn't so bad," Nuell said. "I kind of like it. It would be nice if we had some marshmallows."

"Yes," Weddy said. "That's what I wish we had—hot dogs and marshmallows." She gave me a look. "Only you and Char would get into a fight over how to cook the marshmallows. Char would want to make his nice and brown and even, and you would want to just burn it and eat the burnt part and burn it again."

"The burnt part's best," Nuell said.

"You're just saying that because you're too lazy to cook it right," I said.

"Look at you two guys," Weddy said. "You're getting into a fight over how to cook marshmallows and we don't even have any."

We laughed. So it wasn't just the food, I thought. It was the being together, or whatever you called it, that was making us feel cheerful. Something occurred to me. "Maybe it's because we hunted together that's making Handy more friendly," I said. "He might be more willing to help us find the professor now." I knew I ought to call him "your father," instead of "the professor," but I hated the idea that he was their father and not mine. "We have to get across to him the idea that the professor isn't his enemy, even though he cut him that one time."

"That's a pretty hard idea to get across," Nuell said.

"Well, we've got a few more words now," I said. I took out my little notebook and began jotting them down. "There's 'ka.' We know now that it isn't just an angry expression. He used it in a calmer way about the hipparion so it has to mean something like 'hit,' or 'kill,' or 'attack.' Then there's the warning signal, 'bek.' Let's say it means 'look out.' Then we've got the two new ones, 'maymo,' and 'gar.' 'Gar' we're pretty sure means 'friend' or 'buddy' or something like that. 'Maymo' is harder."

"It could be just a victory cry," Weddy said. "The way we would say, 'Yippee,' if we found out we'd won a lottery or something."

"It could be," I said. "It might mean something, though. Like 'We won,' or 'We did it.' "

"Or just 'meat,' " Nuell said.

We were silent, thinking. By now Handy was completely at home with the fire, and he lay down about ten feet from it, curled up and went to sleep, feeling safe and full.

Finally, Weddy spoke. "I'm really getting worried about Dad now. If he were going along in front of us it seems to me that we would have come on some sign of him. You'd think he'd have tried to leave us some mark to show which way he'd gone. He could have ripped a piece off his handkerchief and dropped it. Or he even could have written us a note on a page from his notebook and left it for us. At least you'd think we'd see a footprint or something."

It had been worrying me, too, that we hadn't come on anything. But I didn't want to jump to any hasty conclusion. "Weddy, there's an awful lot of land out here. He could drop a hundred notes and we might miss them. They might not have traveled right along the lake—they could have gone inland a ways and we'd never see any sign of him."

"But what about this campsite?" she said. "They must have come through here."

"Maybe not," I said. "Maybe this isn't their camp at all. Maybe it belongs to a hostile tribe and they had to skirt around it."

"That's another thing," she said. "With all this fighting going on, why wouldn't they kill him?"

I didn't know how to answer that. I was getting the feeling that the longer it took us to find Professor Joher, the worse his chances were. Weddy was right about one thing—these hominids were belligerent toward each other. They seemed to see each other as just animals, to be killed if they felt like it. I was afraid that the ones who had captured Professor Joher would see him that way, too—a kind of interesting new species whom they'd puzzle over for a while and then kill.

But I didn't want to say this to Weddy and Nuell. The main thing was to stay as hopeful as possible and keep on looking. "Well, yes, Weddy, there's always a chance that they might kill him, but I don't think they will."

"Why not?" Nuell demanded. "What's to keep them from doing it?"

I didn't have a very good answer to that, either. "He can be useful to them," I came up with. "He knows a lot of things they would want to know." But it wasn't a very good explanation.

"What are we going to do then?" Weddy asked.

I thought about it for a minute. "The thing I'd like to try is to let Handy take the lead. He knows where his people are likely to be and he's bound to head for them. He's only sticking with us for safety. If somehow we could get him to go first, he'll take us right to your father, I'm sure of it."

"But how—"

At that moment, there was a shout from behind us. We jumped up and swung around. There, standing at the top of the bank of the dry riverbed, were six naked hominid males, about five feet tall. Each held a spear in one hand, a rock in the other. Their muzzles were fairly flat, their bodies muscled and sinewy, and they were wet with sweat, as if they had been running across the hot savannah. I knew at once that they were habilines like Handy—a party of hunters away from the main band. Were they Handy's tribe? If not, they could be very dangerous, a lot more dangerous than the ramapithecines or the australopithecines. They had real weapons that they knew how to use. Our electro-prods weren't going to be much use against men armed with spears.

9.

Handy woke up instantly. He took one look at the line of habilines on the bank and began to limp across to the opposite side of the campsite as fast as he could, shouting, "Bek, bek," at the top of his lungs. Weddy, Nuell and I drew together in the middle of the campsite. I was scared, and I could tell they were, too.

"They aren't Handy's people, that's for sure," Nuell said in a low voice.

"They must have smelled the smoke from our fire," I said. I wondered why we were talking in low voices.

"Or else this is their camp," Weddy said.

"Maybe both," I said.

Up on the bank, the habilines began to shout and

brandish their spears. "I think we ought to leave before there's trouble," Weddy said.

They would begin to throw stones pretty soon, I knew. But even though I was scared, I was curious, too, and I didn't want to leave. I wanted to see what kind of signals they would give each other, or if they had verbal commands. "Let's wait a minute and see what they do," I said.

"Char, please," Weddy said. "Let's go."

"It's a threat display," I said. "It's fascinating. It's the same as two groups of howler monkeys meeting in the forest and howling at each other. Or a chimpanzee baring his teeth at a rival. Or a silverback gorilla pounding on his chest and roaring. They won't attack yet. They'll display for a while first, until they work themselves up into a mood to fight."

"Char, it's stupid to take a chance," she said.

"I want to see if I can talk to them, Weddy. We've got some words now. We might be able to make them understand that we're friendly."

"Maybe they don't understand Handy's language," Nuell said.

He was right, although I hated to admit it. It was a smart idea. Even though they were the same species they might come from a different tribe and speak a different language. "It's worth a try," I said.

Two of the habilines were now sliding down the embankment into the dry riverbed, watching us cautiously and holding their spears in front of them with both hands, ready to fight in case we attacked.

"Char," Weddy said. "Let's go."

"Wait a minute, Weddy," I said. "I want to try to talk to them." I gave Nuell a quick look. I figured he might be willing to take a chance for the excitement in it. "Don't you think it's worth a try, Nuell?"

He looked at the habilines. "I think we ought to stop fooling around and try to find Dad."

He was right about that, too. I was torn: I knew we should be looking for the professor, but I wanted to see if I could communicate with the habilines, too. It's what Professor Joher would have done. He wouldn't have missed a chance like this for anything. But Weddy and Nuell were outvoting me. And it occurred to me that we would be better off facing them up on the top of the other bank, rather than down in the riverbed. "Okay," I said. "Let's pull back to the other bank, but let's not run. That'll only draw them after us."

We turned and walked quickly back across the riverbed, watching the hunting party over our shoulders as we did so. When we reached the opposite bank we scrambled up it and stood at the top, looking down into the campsite.

One of the habilines had gone to the lake and was kneeling to drink. Two had stopped to examine the remains of the hipparion. One of them, in fact, had picked up a bone and was gnawing at it. The others, however, were coming slowly toward us, wary, but confident that they had us outnumbered and could drive us away. I was scared by what I was about to do, but excited, too. I would have to be careful—but I knew that I was smarter than they were.

"Come on, Char, let's go," Nuell said. "We have to find Dad." He gave me a look and then he turned and marched off into the grass.

"You guys go," I said. "I'll come in a minute."

"Char," Weddy said. Suddenly she was very angry. "You're just trying to start another fight," she shouted. "I thought we were finished fighting for a while."

It worried me that she was mad at me. "I'm not trying to start a fight, Weddy. I want to see if I can talk to them."

"You're getting them mad," she shouted. "Can't we just go away?"

I hated her to be mad at me, but I didn't want to be bossed around, either. "You go. I'll come in a minute."

She swung her head wildly from side to side as if she were looking for an escape route. "I can't stand any more fighting," she said. Then she turned and went off through the tall grass after Nuell. In a moment she caught up with him.

I watched them go, then I turned back to the habilines in the dry riverbed. Four of them had come to within seventy-five or a hundred feet of me and stood there, once more gesturing angrily with their spears. I turned to look at Handy. He had limped out into the tall grass a couple of hundred feet and stood there shouting, "Bek, bek." He was plenty scared of the other hunters. I wondered if he recognized them as people he'd fought against before or was just scared of strangers in general.

Suddenly, one of the hunters threw a stone. I jumped aside. A second stone sailed up toward me and I ducked again.

In a moment they were now throwing stones steadily, and I was kept busy ducking. They were much better throwers than the australopithecines. Instead of facing the target as they threw they had learned to turn sideways, as we did. I figured it might have taken a million years for humans to learn this little trick. If the chimpanzees had ever learned it they might have taken over the world, instead of us.

What worried me most was having some of them slip around behind me to cut off my retreat. Once they had me trapped they'd be able to kill me easily. But at the moment they seemed more interested in driving me away than in attacking. I guess that I looked pretty strange and frightening, and they were not sure what they'd get into if they attacked. But sooner or later they would, if they couldn't drive me away.

Now I raised my hand, palm outward, in the universal gesture of peace. "Gar," I said loudly, using the word for "friend" Handy had given us. "Gar."

Suddenly startled, they stopped throwing stones and stood staring up at me. "Gar," I said. I was feeling very nervous, and I wished I had another word to add to it. I waited.

They stared, and they turned to mutter among themselves. Behind them, the two who had remained to investigate the dead hipparion were kneeling and staring at me, too. Finally, one of the spearsmen leaned forward, spat on the ground, shook his spear at me and shouted, "Teegar."

A thrill went up my back. I had a new word. I wanted to keep them talking. I went on holding my palm upright. "Gar, gar."

There was another silence and then some cries, "Teegar, teegar," and a shaking of spears.

It wasn't working. I was feeling very tense and sweaty. "Gar," I said once more.

"Teegar," they shouted. Now they began throwing stones again, and I began to duck.

"Gar, gar." But it was no good. They went on throwing stones. In a minute they would charge, I was sure. So I turned and began to trot off through the tall grass after the others, looking over my shoulder every few seconds to make sure that the hunters weren't coming after me. But they didn't chase me. They were satisfied with just driving me off. The others were standing in the plain about a half mile ahead, waiting for me to come up. Weddy gave me a hard look, but nobody said anything.

We began walking across the plain, keeping in

sight of the lake. We no longer had much choice about where we were going. We couldn't turn back for the spaceship unless we made a long loop around the river-bed campsite. We had to just hope that Handy's band, with Professor Joher, was up ahead of us someplace.

And it seemed they must be. The interesting thing was that Handy was no longer tagging behind us the way he had been. Now he was limping along in front of us. I wasn't sure what had happened between him and us, but something had—something to do with hunting together and eating together and being chased together out of the campsite by the enemy band. He had joined us—or I guess, to be honest, we had joined him. And now he had decided he was the leader. I didn't know if he had figured it out that he knew his way around the plains and we didn't, or if he just wanted to be the leader. But that's what he was now. And I was willing to risk that he was taking us to where his band was camped.

Still, we couldn't be sure. He could be leading us into a trap, he could be doing anything. But whatever it was, it would give me a pretty good chance to learn some more of his language. I'd been thinking about the new word the enemy hunters had given me—"teegar." At first it had sounded to me like one word, "teegar," meaning "enemy." But I was getting another idea, which was different, and excited me. Maybe it was two words, "tee" and "gar." "Gar," I was pretty sure, meant "friend." So what did "tee" mean? If "tee gar" was two words instead of one? In that case it obviously was some kind of negative, meaning "no" or "not" or "un." It was a very important word, because it instantly doubled our vocabulary of Habilese. If "bek" meant "look out" or "danger," so "tee-bek" could be used for "no danger," or "safe." And if "ka" meant "strike," "attack" or "kill," "tee-ka" could be taken to mean "don't attack" or "don't hurt."

But more important, having a negative meant that the habilines could deal with concepts. Their language wasn't just a set of names they applied to things—it had at least a rudimentary syntax, with grammatical rules. It was a very important thing to know.

The sun, now high in the sky above us, was baking hot and drenching us with sweat. Every hour or so we stopped, went down to the lake, stripped off and cooled ourselves down in the water. We wanted to go swimming, but we were scared of the crocodiles. Still, just splashing helped.

Once, down at the water, Weddy coaxed Handy in to check out the wound in his foot. It was covered with dirt and bits of grass. Carefully, Weddy washed the foot out. Handy whimpered, but somehow he realized that she was doing him a favor and he let her do it. Crouching beside him as he stood over her, she said, "It's awfully tender. I hope it isn't getting infected." Handy stared down at her, and began to explore her hair softly with his fingers. She looked up at him and his hand fell away. "What was he doing?" she said.

"Grooming," I said. "Searching for dirt and lice. You've seen chimps groom each other. It helps them to keep their fur clean and the bugs off their skin, but it has a social significance, too. It's kind of like the way we hug—it's a sign of affection."

She stood up, not sure how to take that. "You mean Handy was being affectionate to me?"

"Sure," I said. "Why not? When you were cleaning his cut it was like grooming to him."

We went on walking through the heat all the rest of the day. We tried to stay as close to the lake as we could. It was safer there because we couldn't be ambushed in the open space of the beach. But sometimes the shoreline rose up in a rock cliff, and we had to swing inward until the ground fell again.

Also, we kept hoping we'd see the professor's footprints in the pebbly sand. We figured that if they were really going in this direction the habilines would walk along the beach the way we were doing, at least sometimes. A couple of times we came to places where the sand was kicked up. We figured that a band of some kind had come down to the lake to drink, or maybe cool off in the water. But they'd disturbed the sand so much that there weren't any individual footprints visible. We had no way of knowing whether the professor had been with them, or even if it had been a habiline band at all.

We went on walking and looking and hoping, and after a while the sun drifted over to the horizon in the west, and we realized that we weren't going to find

Professor Joher that day and we'd better start looking for a place to sleep for the night.

We stopped by the lakeside and sat with our feet in the water, feeling worried and tired and depressed. Handy sat nearby, frowning and poking at the sand with a piece of stick. He wanted to keep going and he was impatient with us, but we needed a rest.

"What if we can never get out of here?" Weddy said.

"We wouldn't last very long," Nuell said.

"Don't be so pessimistic, Nuell," I said.

"I'm not being pessimistic, I'm being realistic," he said bluntly. "We wouldn't last very long." He stared at me, challenging me. "We don't know anything about this place. We don't know how to hunt and we don't have any weapons."

"We can make weapons," I said. "We can easily make spears. We can make them by charring the end of a stick and scraping it to a point. The fire hardens the tip." We were arguing again.

"What good would a spear be against one of those big cats? They'd pick us off one by one."

"We chased off the smilodon," I said.

Suddenly Weddy flung her hands over her ears. "Stop it," she shouted. "I can't stand it, I can't stand it, I can't stand it."

I looked at Nuell and Nuell looked at me. Nobody said anything. Then Nuell said, "Char always thinks he's the boss." He was sore.

"Well, I should be," I said. I was sore, too. "I'm older than you and I know more than you do. If you studied harder instead of goofing around you'd know this stuff, too."

He jumped up. He was good and angry now. "You study all the time just to impress Dad. You want to be the big star with him."

I jumped up, too. "That's a lie," I shouted. But I knew that it wasn't. It was what I wanted—to get Professor Joher to like me best. I wanted to hear him say to me, "Char, Nuell's a good boy, but I count on you," or something like that. He'd never said it. I began to feel hot and blush. I didn't say anything, but stood facing Nuell, getting red.

Then Nuell said, "I'm sorry, Char. I didn't mean to say it."

I looked down at the ground. I felt confused. Nuell felt sorry for me because I didn't have a father—or even a family, really. But he was right about it, and if he had apologized to me, I had to admit it. "No, you're right, Nuell."

Weddy was standing up, too, looking at both of us, "Why do you fight all the time?" she said. "Why?"

"I don't know," Nuell said. "It seems like everything Char does makes me sore." He stopped. "No, not everything. Only when he gets bossy."

I could understand that. Nobody likes to be bossed around. Still, I thought I had a right to be the boss. But it would only cause more trouble if I said that. "I don't mean to be bossy," I said.

"You probably don't," Nuell said. "But you are."

I looked at Weddy. "Nuell's right, Char," she said.

That hurt. Was I really that bossy? I felt like everybody was against me and I had to fight back. "But what am I supposed to do when I know about something?"

Nobody said anything. Everything that had been said was true, and we were stuck. Then Nuell said, "I don't really want to keep arguing with you all the time, Char. I just feel like I have to."

I could understand that, too. And I knew he was trying to get rid of the problem between us by admitting he shouldn't argue so much, even if he couldn't help it. Suddenly, I felt sort of relaxed and not so angry any more. "Okay," I said, "I'll try not to be so bossy."

Handy was still sitting in the sand watching us and looking puzzled. Now he rose up, grabbed Weddy firmly by the arm and said, "Doy."

"He wants us to get going," Weddy said. "Maybe he's taking us someplace safe to sleep."

"We can't be sure of that," I said. " 'Doy' could mean anything. Maybe he just wants you to groom him again."

"Doy," Handy said again, tugging at Weddy's arm. "Doy."

"No, Char," Nuell said. "Look at him. He's trying to pull her toward the grass. He wants us to get going."

He was right. We stood. Handy dropped Weddy's

arm and limped quickly into the savannah grass, look-ing back over his shoulder as he did so to see if we were following. When he saw that we were coming behind him, he headed off across the savannah toward the setting sun. "I hope he knows what he's doing," Nuell said. "I'd hate to have to spend the night out here in the middle of the plain."

We went on for fifteen minutes, and then Handy stopped and pointed toward the sun, which was begin-ning to touch the distant horizon of grass and acacia trees. There, perhaps two miles in the distance, was a rock outcropping a quarter of a mile long which rose maybe a hundred feet above the surface of the plain. From that distance it looked like a jumble of rock covered with patches of brush. There was a grove of trees of some kind on the top. "There must be caves or something up in there," Weddy said.

We began walking toward it. As we got closer, we could see that the rock face slanted up steeply. There was at least one cave in it that I could see, although I couldn't tell how deep it was. We kept on walking, and in a few minutes we were standing in the shadow of it, looking up.

The outcropping was a piece of tilted ledge which had been squeezed up out of the earth by enormous pressure and then eroded by millions of years of wind and rain. It was cut with crevices and now I could see there were several shallow caves in the rock face. Flocks of birds wheeled around the top, settling for the night, and near one end a band of theropithecus baboons sat on a series of shelflike ledges, looking at us nervously.

Handy began to climb the rocks, and we climbed after him. It was an easy climb. There was a kind of pathway of natural hand- and footholds. I figured that various kinds of hominids had been going up and down that cliffside for thousands of generations, and they'd worn footholds into the rock from use. It was even possible, I realized, that some habiline group had hacked footholds into the rock deliberately. I doubted it, though; the cliff face was rough and there were enough places to grip anyway.

In less than five minutes we were at the mouth of the largest of the caves. It was about two-thirds of the way up the cliff and not very big—about fifteen feet deep and only six or eight feet at the widest place. A band of ten or fifteen people would have been pretty crowded sleeping in it, but if you put a couple of spearmen at the mouth they would be able to fend off a jaguar.

We climbed into the cave and had a look around. The floor was covered with stones, dried bones, feathers, bits of eggshell, even fish bones. "They must hole up here during bad weather," Nuell said. "When it's raining or something."

Weddy hunkered down and began to pick through the debris. "Look," she said. "Nutshells." She picked one up and examined it. "It's fairly fresh. Somebody's been here recently."

"Maybe it was Handy's bunch with Dad," Nuell said hopefully.

"Could have been," I said. "It's hard to tell."

"No, no," Nuell said suddenly. "It must have been. That's why we didn't find any tracks along the shore. They were heading right for this place, so they were traveling inland."

It made sense, and I was annoyed with myself for not thinking of it first. "What about those scuff marks where they came down to the beach to drink?"

"That could have been an entirely different batch," Nuell said.

"Well, you could be right," I said.

"I know I'm right," Nuell insisted. "Let's look and see if there's any sign of Dad."

Handy was already searching around in the debris for something to eat. We stooped beside him and began sorting through the litter for signs of Professor Joher. "He might even have left us a note," Weddy said.

I didn't believe that. Professor Joher had no way of knowing that we'd ever be in that particular cave. It was too much of a long shot. In fact, he had no way of knowing that we'd be following him at all. What would be the point of leaving a note? But I didn't say anything.

"I found a nut," Weddy said suddenly. She held it up. The shell was thick and soft, like a butternut. She put it in her mouth, cracked the shell with her teeth and tasted the meat. "Good," she said. "I wouldn't mind a handful for supper."

"They must have come from right around here someplace," Nuell said. "It would be rough carrying a lot of nuts from a long distance unless they had a basket or something."

"No," I said. "I don't think they had any kind of containers. You don't begin to get pottery making until really late. The nuts must come from close by."

"Let's ask Handy," Weddy said. He had found a fresh bone, and with a small chopper he had picked up out of the mess on the cave floor, he was splintering it to get at the marrow. Weddy nudged him on the arm with the part of the nut she hadn't eaten. "Any more of these around, Handy?"

He stared at her quizzically. Then he took the nut and turned it over in his hand, inspecting it. Once again, Weddy pantomined eating. Finally, Handy gave her back the piece of nut, limped quickly to the mouth of the cave and disappeared upward. We went to the cave mouth and craned our necks around to look. Handy was going rapidly up the cliffside and in a moment he disappeared over the top.

We sat down at the cave mouth to wait. It was growing darker. On the plain below us black pools were spreading in the low places and the herds of animals were feeding quietly. We could see antelopes there and a herd of elphas, and giraffes and a pack of baboons moving slowly toward us, probably coming to sleep for the night on ledges on the rock face. "It's beautiful, isn't it?" Weddy said after a minute. "I just wish we could find Dad. It would be so wonderful if he were here with us."

"The animals," Nuell said. "That's what gets me. There's just so much of everything. I love to see them out there just doing what they do."

We were silent, thinking. Finally, Weddy said, "Don't you think it's beautiful, Char?"

She wanted me to like it the way she did, but I was different. "Well, not so much beautiful as exciting," I said. "I mean, I don't see it the way you do. What I see is how it all works, how the whole thing meshes together —the ungulates eating the grass and the carnivores preying on the ungulates and the snakes eating birds' eggs and the hominids eating snakes' eggs and eventually everything going back to the earth again to fertilize the grass. It all meshes together in this terribly complicated way, and it works. It goes on and on and on for millions and millions of years, changing and shifting little by little as the land shifts and the climate alters, so that after a while you have a whole different thing, with maybe lush jungle where you once had plains, and different species of animals. But still it goes on working. That's what's beautiful to me—to see it fit together in this incredible way. And if you go in there and change something, just some little thing like bringing in a new bacterial form or killing off the water birds, you can mess the whole thing up and it won't work any more."

Suddenly, we heard scraping sounds and in a minute Handy dropped down into the cave mouth. He was carrying a double handful of nuts. It must have been an awkward climb back down the cliff face with his hands full. "He sure took a lot of trouble over it," Nuell said.

Handy threw Nuell and me a quick look. Then he walked up to Weddy and held out his cupped hands with the nuts in them. "Riwi," he said.

Weddy looked at us. "He wants me to take them," she said.

"Take them," I said. "Let's see what happens."

She took the nuts, clutching them to herself so she wouldn't drop them. She smiled at him. "Thanks, Handy."

He grinned. "Riwi," he said again.

"That's what he said when he gave you the meat before," I said in a low voice.

Now Handy was bending his head toward her. "What's he doing?" Nuell said.

" I don't know," I said.

Weddy looked back at us. "I don't like this," she said. "Do you think I should share the nuts with you guys?"

"No," I said. "He wants you to have them. Better just eat them. We can go up ourselves later and get some more if we want."

Weddy started to stoop to put the nuts down on the cave floor, but before she could move very far, Handy grabbed her arm, gripping it firmly. "Riwi," he said.

She straightened up and looked at us again. She was unnerved, I could see that. "Char—" Once again, Handy bent his head toward her.

"Be careful, Weddy," I said. I was worried. I knew how fast he could strike when he wanted. "Don't do anything sudden."

Now Handy took her hand and began to tug it toward him. "I don't know what he wants," she said, her face still fearful.

"Relax your arm and see what he does with your hand."

She let her arm go limp. Handy drew it toward him and placed it on the black hair of his head. "He wants you to groom him," Nuell said.

"That's what it is, Weddy," I said.

"Oh," she said. "Well, if that's all. Okay, Handy." She began to pick through his hair. He stood in front of her with his head bent, a smile on his face. In a moment his eyes closed. "He sure could use a shampoo," Weddy said. She went on grooming him for a few minutes, and then stopped and withdrew her hand. "That's enough, Handy," she said. Instantly, he grabbed her hand and replaced it on his hair.

"I think he's in love with her," Nuell said.

I knew at once he was right. It was some kind of a courtship ritual. He wanted Weddy for his girlfriend, or mate, or wife—whatever it was that they had. Suddenly, I felt my stomach knot, and I knew I was jealous and angry at him for trying to take away my girl. What right did he have to fool around with her? She was mine, she wasn't his. Then I realized that I was being silly. Besides, what gave me the idea that she was my girl anyway?

Weddy went on grooming Handy and I sat and watched. It was fascinating to see how something like grooming could come down the generations to us from these early hominids. We didn't groom each other, exactly. But if people you cared for were hurt, or tired, or unhappy over something, you would touch them to comfort them—put your arm around their shoulders or pat them, or rub their cheek a little.

And as I watched it occurred to me that there was one of our words that Handy might really want to know. That was "Weddy." I went over to where she was bent over Handy, her hand combing through his hair. I poked her lightly on the shoulder. "Weddy," I said.

Handy looked at me and his brows above the big eyebrow ridges furrowed. He didn't like my interrupting. Maybe he thought I was trying to take Weddy away. "Weddy," I said.

He made a low growl. "Gar, Handy," I said. Then I touched Weddy again.

He made the same low growl.

"You better stop," Weddy said. "He doesn't get it."

I stepped back and looked at Handy. "I think he gets it," I said. "He just doesn't want anybody fooling around while you're grooming him." I didn't know why I felt that he understood about Weddy's name, but I felt it just the same.

10.

In the morning, as soon as there was enough light, we climbed down the rock face, walked back across the plain to the lake and continued on along the shore in the direction we'd been going.

Handy was still taking the lead. If anything, he'd become more sure of his place. When we slowed or wanted to stop to rest or cool off in the lake, he'd get impatient after a few minutes and start shouting, "Doy, doy." The funny thing was, we grumbled, but after a few minutes one of us would say, "He's getting sore, we'd better go," as if we were privates in the army and he were the sergeant.

I wasn't sure that I liked having him take over that way. When I was a kid and first went to work for Professor Joher, I'd been sort of awed by the whole Joher family. I mean, I was fresh out of the slums, I didn't know anything about music or painting or politics or philosophy or anything like that. They'd sit around at dinner talking about some concert they were going to, or the newest philosophic idea, and I'd think they were far smarter than I could ever be—some special kind of beings.

Of course, they had books all around the house on the things they talked about, like art and politics, and I began to borrow them and read them at night out in my little room in the laboratory. And as I got to know the Johers better, I realized that they weren't quite all geniuses. To tell the truth, Nuell didn't really know much about any of that stuff. He was more interested in sports than in reading, and most of what he learned he picked up from conversations at dinner.

Weddy, of course, was a good student. But she had a lot of friends and things to do, and I didn't—I didn't have any friends at all, so I could study all the time, and I caught up with her pretty fast. I even discovered that the professor could make mistakes—not in archeology, of course, but in other things. Once he gave a quote from Plato that I knew was from Aristotle, and another time he confused Handel's *Messiah* with Bach.

So I caught up, and after a while Weddy and Nuell realized that I was going ahead of them, and things changed. They started looking up to me and after a while I became the leader.

So I didn't really like having Handy take over the way he was doing. I didn't like Weddy to see me lose my rank. It annoyed me; it made me a little sore with Handy. First he'd tried to get Weddy to be his girlfriend, and now he had decided to run things.

But still, even if it did annoy me, I knew that it was best to let him lead so he could find sleeping places for us and, I hoped, take us to where Professor Joher was. In the end, I knew I could beat him if I had to. He was probably stronger than I, because he'd been running and fighting on these plains all of his life, while I'd been reading books. But I was a lot smarter and bigger, and I had the electro-prod. I could win if I wanted to.

We walked on up the lakeshore. Sometimes the beach disappeared into the papyrus swamp, sometimes it narrowed down to nothing when the shore rose up into a cliff, and we'd have to move out into the tall grass. The sun, once it got up, was hot as ever, and we sweated most of the time and stopped as often as Handy would let us to cool off in the lake. When we stopped, Weddy would usually wash his foot off. She was worried about it because it was raw and puffy. "He shouldn't be walking around on it," she said. "He should stay off it."

"There's no way you could make him do that," Nuell said. "Look at him. We've only been here five minutes and he wants to go already."

Handy stood on the beach, frowning. "Doy," he said, gesturing away from the water.

The second time this happened we had hardly

stepped into the water before Handy started hollering "Doy, doy." Weddy and I were out splashing ourselves off. Nuell was sitting by the shore, soaking his feet.

"He's pretty bossy, isn't he?" Weddy said.

"He's the leader now," I said. Suddenly, I decided to ask her something I'd been wondering about all morning. "Listen, did you mind it when Handy made you groom him last night?" I knew I wanted her to say she hadn't liked it.

"No, I didn't mind," she said.

I was disappointed. "You didn't mind at all?"

"Why should I?" she said. "He's supposed to be our friend now."

"I thought you would have minded, is all."

She stared at me for a minute. Then she said, "Char, you're jealous of Handy."

I began to blush and cursed myself for giving my feelings away. "No, I'm not," I said.

"Yes, you are," she said.

I felt myself going hot and prickly. "Well, what of it?"

"You shouldn't be jealous of people all the time, Char."

I kept on blushing. "Why not? If I like you, why shouldn't I be jealous?" It was the first time I'd actually said anything like that to her, although I always figured she knew anyway.

Now she got red. "Oh, you shouldn't be jealous of Handy. It was more like brushing a dog or a horse."

But she went on blushing and I knew, suddenly, that she didn't want me to be mad at her. I grinned. "Yeah, sure, Weddy," I said.

"Oh, come on, Char." She bent over and splashed her face with water, and I knew it was to stop blushing. I felt good and I went on grinning. I wasn't sure why, exactly, but I knew that someday I would try to kiss her, and she'd let me.

"Doy, doy," Handy began shouting.

"Okay, Handy, we're doying," Nuell said. As we climbed out of the lake and began walking again, I wondered about Handy. What really went on in his head? Did he really have as much intelligence as I thought he did? Could he figure anything out? Or was he just a smart animal—a kind of super-chimpanzee who could manage rudimentary tools and hunt, but who couldn't really think things over and make decisions about them?

I knew that the smarter primates, especially the great apes like chimps and gorillas, led complicated social lives. They lived in groups the way hominids did. The groups had their leaders and their followers. Some were smarter than others, some lazier, some crosser and more quick to fly off the handle. In that way, chimps were a lot like people.

But modern humans were basically a lot smarter and more able to think through a course of action instead of just leaping into something. And how did Handy fit in? Was he more like the chimps or more like us?

What I particularly wondered was what he thought of us. He'd made friends with us—or to be more accurate, the four of us had formed into a little hominid band. We had leaders and followers, and we looked out for each other. But what did it really mean to Handy? And how would he behave when he ran into his own kind? Would he tell them that we were his friends and not to attack us? Or would he go against us? It was hard to tell, but I figured that sooner or later we were going to find out.

The ground ahead of us was now beginning to rise, at first slanting upward easily and then angling up more sharply, to make a kind of cliff along the lakeshore. In a few minutes the beach disappeared and we were walking up a sloping hillside. As the grassy slope got steeper and steeper, we began to sweat. There were no trees on the slope at all—I figured it was all rock right underneath the topsoil, and the trees couldn't put roots down there. It seemed like a long way to the top. We just kept plugging onward until we were drenched in sweat and our legs were tired, and then we stopped to lie down in the grass.

But Handy wouldn't let us. "Doy, doy," he shouted.

"Tee-doy," Weddy said.

"Doy, doy."

"He's really eager to go," Weddy said.

"Maybe we're getting close," Nuell said.

We looked at each other. If that were true, we'd know soon whether the professor was dead or alive. It made us all fall silent. Finally, Nuell said, "Okay, let's go."

We got up out of the dusty grass we had been lying in and began walking again. And we'd only gone a couple of steps when we heard distant sounds—a kind of faint bellow, like an elephant trumpeting, followed by high yips.

Handy stopped dead still and stood with his head cocked, listening carefully to the sounds. Then suddenly he began to sprint up the hill as fast as he could go with the limp. We began to run after him, but even with his limp he was going faster than we were. There was still a quarter of a mile to go to the top. Handy went on running, getting smaller and smaller, until he disappeared over the top. We went running on, and then we came to the crest.

"Down," I said. We dropped to the ground and lay there, peering through the tall grass down the other slope. Handy was already halfway down the other side of the hill, running with that limping trot. At the bottom of the hill there was a large band of habilines by the lakeside, maybe twenty-five or thirty of them. They had driven a deinotherium into the papyrus swamp off the shore, and they were attacking from the beach. The huge animal, with its down-curving tusks, was sunk up to its knees in the mucky bottom, and was struggling to pull its legs up out of the suction of the mud. Every once in a while it threw back its giant head, those huge tusks flashing in the sun, and trumpeted.

On shore, a group of females and younger males were stoning the animal, trying to strike it around the face and eyes. The older males, equipped with spears, were out among the papyrus reeds, nearly up to their waists in the water, trying to get in close enough to the deinotherium to jab it. They'd wade forward and take a stab, and then the deinotherium would sweep its tusks back to try to get in a hit, and the hominids would dive back out of reach. With their lighter weight, they were able to keep from sinking in the muck, but the deinotherium was stuck.

Even so, the habilines were having a hard time killing it. Its hide was so tough and thick that the spears mostly slid off it, as if it were slippery metal. But they had managed to work a hole about three inches in diameter into the animal's flesh at the belly, and they kept wading in and stabbing at it to make it larger. A little stream of blood was trickling from it. But it was a pretty small wound in an animal of that size, and the deinotherium was full of fight. I realized that if it could manage to break its legs out of the muck it would charge through the habiline band, smashing people left and right with its trunk and tusks.

We stared at the sight, feeling surprised, and then suddenly Weddy shouted, "Look, it's Dad." She pointed. Professor Joher was sitting in the grass back from the action, watching and making notes. His shirt was torn and drifting down his shoulder, but otherwise he didn't seem hurt.

A great feeling of relief came over me. The three of us looked at each other. "Thank God he's safe," Weddy said. I could see tears starting at the corners of her eyes and I felt like crying myself. "It's wonderful," I whispered.

"Let's go," Nuell said. He started to his feet, but I grabbed him by the legs and dumped him down to the ground again.

"Take it easy, Nuell," I said. "Let's not go rushing down there until we know what the situation is. He still may be a prisoner."

Nuell knelt up to stare over the tall grass. "He can't be, Char. Look, he's just sitting there making notes. Come on, let's go."

"Hang on, Nuell," I said. "Let's wait."

"I think Nuell's right," Weddy said. "I don't think he's a prisoner. He's just been following along with the band, studying them."

I still wasn't sure. They wanted to be with their dad so badly they didn't want to think about anything else. I wanted to be with him, too, but I knew we should play it safe. "Please, you guys," I started to say, but just at that moment Handy reached the bottom of the hill. He was immediately surrounded by a bunch of habilines who thronged around him, hugging him.

"Look at that," Nuell said. "Handy's there, he'll tell them we're okay."

Weddy nodded. "You're being too cautious, Char. I think we should go down."

"I'm going," Nuell said.

"Me, too," Weddy said.

"What are we waiting for, then?" Nuell said. Together, the two of them rose out of the concealment of the tall grass and began to run down the hill. I started to rise myself, but then something made me squat back down in the grass. I felt sort of ashamed not to be racing down there to the professor, too, but I still didn't trust the situation.

I watched Weddy and Nuell race downhill through the tall grass. Halfway down they began to shout, "Dad, Dad."

I looked down at Professor Joher. At the shouts, his head snapped around and then he was on his feet, his hands high over his head, waving at them frantically to go back.

Weddy and Nuell were now almost to the bottom. They wavered and stopped. Professor Joher shouted something I couldn't make out and went on waving them back. They turned to flee back up the hill, but a dozen habilines were pouring up the slope after them. Weddy and Nuell ran, but the habilines rolled over them, and then they were just a boiling mass of people in the grass. In a moment, the habilines were dragging Weddy and Nuell back into camp by their arms. I could see the two of them writhing as they were pulled along, trying to raise their bodies up to avoid being scraped on the rough ground. Once Weddy shrieked with pain. The habilines dragged them up to their father and dumped them there.

They fell on him and hugged him, and I knelt in the grass, my heart pounding, feeling sick and miserable. The one thing I realized was that Handy knew I was up there somewhere. He might tell the others, and he might not, but I couldn't take a chance. I was the only one left now; it was up to me to save us all.

Crouching, I slipped away in the tall grass and started down the slope we'd come up. When I'd gone a hundred yards down I stood erect and looked back. There was nobody at the top behind me, so I started to run. I was all alone now and scared and unhappy. I knew that the basic law for hominids was that a lone human being could not survive for very long. You were hunted by cats and snakes and in the water, crocodiles. You had to gather food and water yourself, and it was almost impossible for a lone man to hunt anything. If you got sick, or fell from a cliff and broke a leg or an arm, there was nobody to protect you and care for you while you healed. For ancient man, the rule was that only by sticking together could the species survive. And I knew that everything that human beings were came out of this law— love and rivalry and friendship and war and music and philosophy and even language itself.

And now I was alone and scared, jogging through the plain, jumping at sounds, swiveling my head from side to side all the time, frightened that suddenly I'd see something tawny flash out at me. There was only one place to go where I'd be safe, and that was the cave we'd spent the night in. Later, when I was sure that Handy's band wasn't following me, and I had a chance to think things through and work out a plan, I'd come back and see what the situation was. But for now, all I could think of was getting to someplace safe.

I went on running, until my legs felt weak and my lungs ached and burned, and then I ducked into the lake and kneeled there, resting. Here at least I had a clear view around me, even though there were crocs out there somewhere. For fifteen minutes I rested, and then I got nervous that the habilines might be on my track, and I waded out of the water and began running across the savannah through the tall grass once more, nervous and lonely and swinging my head constantly from one side to the other. Then finally I saw the outcropping appear over to my right, and I headed toward it. Fifteen minutes later I was there.

I climbed up the rocky face and then on past the cave mouth to the top and looked around. It was like standing on the deck of a ship moving through a wide, gray green sea. In the middle of the plateau was a group of trees—the nut trees Handy had gone to the night before. It was food and I walked over to them. They were about twenty-five feet tall with fine leaves. Scattered underneath them were branches and twigs and a good many nuts. There were more nuts hanging in small bunches from the branches. I climbed the tree, which was awkward going with the electro-prod on my back, and sat in the branches for a long time cracking nuts with my teeth and eating them. The view from up there was tremendous. I could see for twenty miles across the plains and way out onto the lake. Everywhere there were animals and it made me forget my troubles. I knew I ought to be watching the area right around me, but I couldn't keep my eyes off the view. It was wonderful.

But then the sun started to go down and the plain to grow black and I was alone in the dark, and the view didn't exhilarate me any more. I was just afraid and sad and worried. How was I going to get out of it? How was I possibly going to free the Johers from the habilines? How was I even going to keep myself alive?

I shivered and climbed down from the tree. The first thing I did was to break a long, straight branch from the nut tree by twisting it around and around until it snapped off. Then I took off my shirt, made a kind of sack out of it by tying the sleeves around the neck hole to close it up and filled it with as many twigs and small dry branches as I could. I climbed down the rocky cliff face, with the branch cocked under one arm and the sack over my shoulder, into the cave where we'd spent the night before. When I was inside, I gathered together some bits of dried leaves and grass. I got them started with the energizer from the electro-prod, and fed in twigs until I had a small fire going. When it was blazing up, I put the frayed end of the branch, where I'd twisted it from the tree, into the flames. I held it there until it was burning, then I stubbed it out on the cave floor. I scraped the charred end on the rough wall of the cave to rub off the charred parts. I did the same thing three or four more times, and finally I had a spear with a sharp, fire-hardened point. I piled some more wood on the fire and lay down at the back of the cave with the electro-prod and the spear beside me. I was pretty exhausted from everything that had happened, and I went right to sleep, even though the sun wasn't yet all the way down.

Some time later I woke up with my heart beating fast. The fire was just smoldering coals. It was night now. From the back of the cave I looked out the cave mouth. Pleisto's two moons were high in the sky and at first I thought that the light shining in had woken me. But then I heard the click of a rock falling and a low growl somewhere right close. My nerves jumped and I tensed. I snatched up the spear, crawled quickly across the cave to the mouth and looked out. I couldn't see anything but the moonlight shining on the rocky cliff face and the plain below. The growl came again; it didn't seem to be more than five feet away, and my scalp went cold.

Quickly, I crawled backward until I was behind the fire. I threw some more branches on it and blew on the smoldering coals until the branches began to blaze, throwing shadows that danced around on the wall. With the spear in my right hand and the prod beside me, I knelt behind the fire and waited. In a minute, a face appeared around the rocky corner of the cave entrance —just two golden eyes set in a black and yellow face.

For a moment, the jaguar and I stared at each other. But I knew I couldn't let it make the first move and I jumped to my feet and shoved the spear toward it. It jerked back its head and disappeared around the corner again. I waited. Once more, I heard the low growl and the face with the golden eyes came back. This time, I could see the muscles of its shoulders rippling under the black and yellow skin. It stretched and yawned, and pushed in some more until its flank was visible, and then its hindquarters, and it was standing before me at the cave mouth. I lunged with the spear. It tipped back and lashed at the spear with a paw. I lunged again, catching it on the shoulder. It snarled again, but it held its ground.

Now, switching the spear to my left hand, I grabbed up a dried branch and shoved it into the fire. In a moment, the twigs on it began to sizzle and blaze. As soon as it was burning well I stood and, holding the spear out in front of me, charged the jaguar. It roared and raised up on its hind legs. I threw the burning branch into its face. It fell backward, confused. As it rolled on the ground, I lunged at it with the spear, catching it hard in the belly. The jaguar yipped, turned, went down the cliffside and disappeared into the shadows of the plain.

For a long time, I sat by the fire, my heart pounding, my legs weak, my palms sweaty, staring out into the darkness. Finally, when I was sure the jaguar was gone, I went to the back of the cave and lay down to sleep.

11.

In the morning I went up the cliff, climbed up into the nut tree and sat there thinking as I ate breakfast. I was feeling a little better than I had the day before. For one thing, fighting off the jaguar during the night gave me some courage: If I did it once, I could probably do it again. For another thing, even with the jaguar's appearance, I'd had a fairly good night's sleep. My stomach was full, too: It took a long time to get enough meat out of the nuts to fill up, and it got boring after a while, but there was plenty of good protein in them, and I knew I'd be okay for a few hours.

So I felt more optimistic than I had when I'd reached the cave the night before. It seemed to me that maybe I could find a way to rescue the Johers after all. I had one big advantage: I was smarter than anybody else on the planet by a good deal. I couldn't outfight them, but I could outthink them.

My first thought was whether I ought to try to fly the spaceship back to earth to get help. It would only take a half-dozen people with modern weapons to rescue the Johers from the habilines. The trouble with that idea was that it would take too much time. The habilines might decide to kill the Johers in the meantime, or they might be killed in some other way—by a jaguar, or die of some Pleistocene disease we didn't have any remedy for.

Besides, there was always the chance that the Committee back on earth would decide not to send out a mission to rescue the Johers. It would be terribly expensive, and they might decide that the Johers would have to be sacrificed, the way soldiers are sacrificed in war.

The thing I kept coming to was what would I do without the Johers? Suppose the habilines killed them and somehow I managed to fly the spaceship out of there, what would be the point of going back? I'd be back in the slums with nobody around me. The Johers were the only people I had. That was my own fault— since I'd started working with Professor Joher I hadn't bothered to make any friends. Partly that was because I was too busy studying and working, and the Johers had been enough; partly it was because I was kind of shy.

So if I went back, I'd be alone again, the way I was before when I was living with my mother. I didn't know if I could stand that. And how could I bear it knowing that Weddy had been murdered, and the professor and Nuell, too? No, somehow I had to find a way to save them. I'd rather take a chance on getting killed myself then go back to a life without them.

Even Nuell. It was true—I was competitive with Nuell, and jealous of him, too. It made me sore that he got everything for nothing, and I had to work for it all. The Johers were his family, they weren't mine. What had he done to deserve a family and me not have one? But even if I were jealous of Nuell, I liked him anyway. It wouldn't stop me from being competitive with him, but I liked him anyway.

The big question, then, was how was I going to rescue them? And would Handy help? It would make an awful lot of difference if he would. What I had to do, at any rate, was to go back to the habiline encampment and look the situation over. I was pretty sure that they hadn't moved on yet. They would stay until they killed the deinotherium and butchered it. They might even stay until they had eaten the big animal, or had gotten sick of eating it.

I filled my pockets with nuts in case I didn't find anything else to eat for lunch, climbed out of the nut tree and went down the rocky cliffside with the prod across my back and the spear in my right hand. Walking through the savannah kept me nerved up and looking around all the time, but once I got to the lakeshore and could go along the beach I felt safer. On the beach I'd be able to spot anything coming and run out into the water, although there was the risk of crocs there. I kept looking around anyway.

It took me two hours to get to the hilltop overlooking the habiline camp. The deinotherium was still standing in the papyrus swamp. It had sunk even farther into the muck with its great weight and the water was now up to its belly. Its head drooped, so that its long, down-curving tusks were half in the water. There was now a big slash ripped in its side. Blood was pumping out of it steadily, and a piece of its guts stuck out, too. On the shore, they'd stopped throwing stones. The females and offspring were mostly sitting, watching and waiting for the moment when they could begin to eat. Out in the water the males were lunging at the animal steadily, pushing their spears against that tough hide and leaning on it to get the blood pumping out faster. Every once in a while, the deinotherium would sort of shudder, trying to heave itself out of the mud, but it was too exhausted now to make it.

The most important thing, though, was that I couldn't see the Johers anywhere. I looked carefully over the campsite. It was just a flat, treeless stretch of plain leading down to a narrow beach and the papyrus swamp. To the left, on the side of the encampment away from the lake, there was a grove of acacia trees and beyond that, the rolling plain. The only place the Johers could be hidden was in the acacia forest, but it didn't seem likely that the habilines would let them go into the woods.

They'd want to keep them out in the open where they could watch them.

So where were they? Had they escaped? There was a chance that they could have just broken and run; most of the males were busy with the deinotherium and it was possible that by just charging off they could have gotten away. But I didn't really believe it. The habilines could easily have run them down on the plains. Probably, being bigger and better coordinated, the Johers could run faster, but the habilines had far more stamina and they would catch them eventually.

Or had the habilines killed them already? I didn't believe that, either. There weren't any signs of it—nobody trotting around with some of their clothes on, no heap of fresh flesh and bones. There wasn't much reason to kill them, anyway, because they were going to have a whole huge deinotherium to eat soon.

So the habilines had taken them someplace else. I thought about that for a minute. Probably they had a cave or something where they could keep prisoners—a place where one or two people could easily guard them. The question was, where?

Handy would know. But was there any way I could get him to tell me? Otherwise, I could go wandering around the plain for days and still never find them.

I scanned the campsite until I spotted Handy. He had a spear, but he wasn't out in the water with the other males. Instead, he was standing on the shore, watching more than anything else. As I watched, he started to walk out into the mucky water of the papyrus reeds and I could see that his limp was worse than ever. His wound hadn't had any attention for a day, and I was pretty sure it had become infected.

I was feeling kind of sore at him. He was supposed to be our friend. We'd saved him from the smilodon, we'd helped him hunt, Weddy had taken care of his foot. He was supposed to be our friend, and as far as I could see, he hadn't done anything to help the Johers. That wasn't how friends were supposed to treat each other. But there was the other side of it, too: These were his people, he'd spent his whole life with them. He knew them a lot better than he knew us, and it would be hard for him to go against them. Suddenly, I despaired. When I looked at it like that, what made me think he'd tell me where the Johers were?

There was a shout from the males surrounding the deinotherium in the water. Its huge head sagged more, and its trunk lay limp. Its tusks were buried down in the muck somewhere. It was totally helpless now and the spear holders were standing right next to it, digging into its flesh.

Then its back legs gave way and the rear of its body sagged into the water. The habilines shouted again. They knew they had it now, and they jabbed more furiously. The animal, its head down, was gasping and shuddering and drooling blood from its huge mouth. But it wouldn't die. It stood doggedly there, its front legs holding its head out of the water, unable to do anything but take punishment.

Finally it went down, falling face forward and twisting to one side. It was so large that it lay half out of the water. "Maymo, maymo, maymo," the habilines shouted. The females and juveniles rushed out into the water and the whole tribe began dancing around the dead body, leaping and shouting and throwing their arms into the air. A dozen of them were up on the body, dancing. They kept shouting, "Maymo, maymo, maymo."

But Handy was not dancing. He was sitting on the shore, with his leg bent so he could examine the cut on his foot. Every once in a while he looked out at the dancers and I could tell he was feeling sad that he couldn't be part of the victory celebration.

The dancing trailed off. The habilines straggled back to land. The males began swiftly to sort through stones on the beach, and in a moment a half-dozen of them were down on their knees, one stone pressed onto a larger one as a kind of anvil, while another chipped an edge into the first one. It was amazing how quickly they could do it. Within fifteen minutes, the first one was slogging back out to the deinotherium and beginning to hack at the flesh around the leg joints. They could do it so fast, I realized, because they'd practiced a lot. They didn't have any kind of carrying baskets or sacks, so they couldn't carry a lot of tools along with them in their travels. They had to make new ones each time, which was why there were always a lot of leftover tools at their campsites. The young ones would watch the old ones do it, and that way the techniques of making stone tools were passed down through the generations.

It was amazing, too, how quickly they could cut something as big as a deinotherium apart. There were six or eight males out on the animal now, hacking at it. Already they'd cut off two of the legs, which floated in the water among the papyrus reeds. Soon they'd have all four legs off, and then they'd begin stripping the flesh from the ribs. On the shore, the females and offspring watched eagerly. Some of the kids were running around and around in circles on the beach in their excitement.

Suddenly, I noticed that Handy had gotten up and was standing, looking around. Then, ignoring everything, he began to limp through the campsite and head out along the beach in the opposite direction from me. I was startled. Why was he leaving just when there was going to be a big feast? It had something to do with his foot, I figured. Maybe he was going someplace to wash it off. Or maybe he was headed for some sort of medicinal leaves, although I didn't really think that the habilines had any real knowledge of herbal medicine.

Then I got it: He was going to Weddy to get her to tend the wound. With his small brain he wouldn't have known exactly what it was that Weddy had done to make his foot feel better; it wouldn't have occurred to him that if he kept it clean and stayed off it for a while it would heal. All he knew was that she made it better; it would be some kind of magic to him.

I was elated; if I followed him, he would take me to her. I looked around. The hill where I was hiding in the grass was a sheer drop down to the water. In the other three directions it sloped off more gradually. I could go back down the way I had come up, swing inland away from the campsite to the grove of acacia trees, go along behind that and then swing back toward the lakeshore once I was out of sight of the camp. Then I could track Handy by staying back in the grass. He wouldn't have any reason to suspect that anyone was following him and with his foot hurting the way it did, he wouldn't be able to make much time. If I hurried, I could catch him.

But I knew I'd better get started. It could be that they'd put the Johers someplace close to the campsite and it wouldn't take Handy long to get there. I turned and slipped back down the hillside through the tall grass. Then, at the bottom, I turned inland and began to run until I reached the acacia woods. I slipped into the shadows. There was not much undergrowth here and no tall grass, and I dodged among the tree trunks until I got to the far side. I stopped and looked carefully out into the savannah. A small herd of pygmy giraffes was moving slowly along the distance and overhead some buzzards were wheeling, obviously attracted by the corpse of the deinotherium. No matter how much the hominids ate, there'd be a feast for scavengers, too—buzzards and jackals and probably smaller hominids, like the australo-pithecines and ramapithecines.

I turned north and ran along the edge of the woods,

always looking around, my spear ready in my right hand. There were snakes here and I figured that sooner or later the big cats would begin to smell fresh meat and start coming around. For about fifteen minutes I ran, slowing down to a walk to catch my breath a couple of times. Going along through that long grass I figured I wasn't doing more than a mile in ten minutes. I decided I'd better go a little farther, so that when I came out onto the beach I'd be well out of sight of the habilines. I went on jogging for another few minutes, and I was just about to turn back into the woods to cut toward the beach when I saw the australopithecines. I ducked into the woods and crouched there in the shadows, looking at them.

They were a half mile away and walking slowly along in a loose pack over an area close to thirty feet square. A couple of the biggest males were out front, with the other males to the sides and rear and the females in the middle. A couple of the women were carrying babies and I figured that down in the grass where I couldn't see them were some juveniles. As they went, they constantly looked around, watching out for predators and at the same time searching for food—eggs, berries, turtles, baby birds, even grubs and beetles.

Were they the same group we'd driven off the island—the group Handy had attacked? They looked like it; it seemed to me that there were about the same number of males and females in it as in the other one. I couldn't be sure, but if it were, they'd really have it in for Handy if they found him. They'd kill him, that was for sure.

I had to get to him first. Limping the way he was, there would be no way for him to escape. They'd fling him to the ground and bash his skull in with stones. I turned and began to dart through the woods as fast as I could, ducking and dodging around the tree trunks. In a couple of minutes I came to the lakeside edge. I stood looking around. There was a stretch of plain about a quarter of a mile wide, and then the lake, with the sunlight winking off the little waves. There was nothing else. I stepped a few feet into the grass and looked back in the direction of the campsite. I couldn't see that, either; the lakeshore turned back here and the camp, the deinotherium and all were out of sight.

I ran through the grass until it ended abruptly at the beach. Once again I stopped, and crouching in the grass, looked down the beach. There was nothing. I turned to look the other way and there was Handy, a good hundred yards away, limping awkwardly over the stony sand.

12

"Handy," I shouted. At the sound of my voice he swung around. Immediately I start to jog up to him. For a moment he watched me come toward him, and then he turned and began to limp off as fast as he could up the beach. I was puzzled: Why was he running away from me? Was he afraid of me, since his people had captured Weddy and Nuell? That was probably it, I figured: He thought I was going to attack him for whatever they had done to them. That was a problem—if he were afraid of me he was likely to be hostile, and unlikely to tell me where the Johers were, assuming they were still alive. "Handy," I shouted. "Gar. Gar, Handy."

He looked quickly over his shoulder, but went on limping on up the beach as fast as he could go. I was gaining on him rapidly, and in a couple of minutes I came up behind him, grabbed him by the shoulder and pulled him to a stop. We stood there facing each other, panting. "Gar, Handy," I said.

He looked down at the ground. "Tee-gar," he muttered.

"Gar," I said. "Tee-ka."

He turned his face away from me. "Tee-gar," he said, this time more firmly.

I stepped around to confront him. "Gar," I said.

He looked away again. "Tee-gar."

He was ashamed of himself and embarrassed for abandoning us. We'd confused all of his loyalties. He knew he owed us something, but he didn't want to be a traitor to his own people. I felt angry at him for letting us down, but I kind of felt sorry for him, too. He was caught in the middle.

But I was determined to get him on our side again. "Weddy," I said. I wished I knew Habilese for "Where is. . . ?" Then I remembered "Doy," which meant something like "Let's get going." That would be clear enough, I figured. "Doy Weddy," I said.

He looked away again. "Tee-doy," he said.

I grabbed his arm again, and tried to make myself sound as commanding as I could. "Doy Weddy, Handy. Doy Weddy."

Suddenly he stiffened and began to stare intently off into the long grass that started at the back edge of the beach. I turned to look. I could see nothing, but Handy had heard or smelled something. It could be one of the big cats, attracted by the smell of the deinotherium; it could be the little australopithecine band. A cat wouldn't worry me—with the prod and the spear we could drive it off. But the australopithecines would be something else. My heart was thumping. We stood there, the two of us, staring down the beach, waiting.

Then they appeared, slipping one at a time out of the tall grass onto the stony beach about fifty yards below us. In a moment they were standing there staring at us. I counted: four males, three females, two subadults. Two of the females were holding babies. It was the same group, all right. One of the males was holding his arm in an awkward fashion: Handy apparently had broken it with his club that night he had attacked them on the island.

Now the males moved to the front of the group and began to threaten, waving their fists and shouting. The females drifted back, with the two subadults flanking them protectively. My heart went on pounding. We had caught them in the water the last time, and at night, when they had no real idea of what they were up against. This time they had us in broad daylight on dry land. They were smaller than us, and more awkward, but they outnumbered us four to two—six to two, if you counted the subadults.

They were shouting louder now, and scooping up stones from the beach. That was another thing: The last time we had the stones; this time they had them, too.

Still, I thought, if we charged them so they wouldn't have much chance with the stones, we could probably drive them off. Aside from the stones they had no weapons, and we had the spear and the electro-prod.

They were edging toward us, and in a moment they began to throw the stones. They were still thirty or forty yards away, and the stones fell short. I looked at Handy. His lips were pulled back in a snarl, and his teeth were bared. He was scared, I could tell that.

I was scared, too. I wished there were some way out of a fight. I wished Handy and I could just make a run for it. But with that cut foot, Handy would never get away from them. We were forced to fight.

Then a stone bounced on the ground in front of me. The australopithecines had edged to thirty yards of us, within the range of their stones. We couldn't wait. If we were going to charge them it would have to be now. "Handy—" I said.

And suddenly he was gone, running up the beach away from the enemy as fast as he could go on his bad foot. "Handy," I shouted again. But he did not even turn to look at me. He knew that the australopithecines would kill him if they caught him, and he was running for his life.

I was alone. The australopithecines were bolder now, and the stones were coming steadily, although not with much force, and I could dodge them. Now what was I going to do? Suddenly, it all seemed hopeless. What was the use of fighting these people? What was the use of trying to save Handy? He wasn't going to tell me where the Johers were anyway. His basic loyalty was to his own tribe, and if they wanted to kill us all, he wouldn't stop them. He had been our ally for a while, but the pull of his own people was too strong. His alliance with us had been temporary, something that came about by chance, and was now over. My shoulders drooped. What was the use of anything?

Then two stones came at me at once. I couldn't duck them both, and one of them banged my shoulder. It stung, and I quickly rubbed the place to see if I had been cut. I didn't have any choice any more. Handy and I together could have driven them away, but alone they could surround me, stone me from all directions, and it would only take a few hits on the head to daze me enough so they could attack. I took one quick look up the beach. Handy was a good distance away, limping as fast as he could go. In a minute he would be almost out of sight around a bend, and perhaps then he could find a place to hide from the australopithecines. Otherwise they would be on him in a minute.

I turned, jumped into the tall savannah grass at the edge of the beach and began to run through it as fast as I could. When I had got a good way in I stopped, turned back and looked. The australopithecines weren't coming after me. But I could hear their shouts in the distance, and I knew that they were racing up the beach after Handy. If they caught him, it would be over in five minutes. They would stone him until he was dazed, charge in and knock him to the ground, and then batter his skull to pieces.

Thinking that, as I stood there in the tall grass, I got a terrible feeling, a sick, sad feeling, the saddest kind of feeling I'd ever had. In the end Handy had gone back on us. He hadn't helped the Johers, and he wouldn't tell me where they were, or even if they were alive. But I couldn't blame him for that. It was the way he was: How could I expect him to go against his own people for some strange creatures he had only known for a couple of days, and couldn't even talk to? But we were friends, Handy and I. Or at least I thought we had been friends. I had liked him and had wanted to know him better. And now, even as I stood there, he was being attacked, and would shortly be dead.

I gritted my teeth. I knew I couldn't stand it, and began to run, first through the tall grass out onto the beach, and then up the beach. Nobody was in sight. Either Handy had ducked off into the tall grass to hide and the australopithecines were searching for him, or they were all around the bend in the beach ahead. I went on running, the sound of my feet on the stony beach loud in my ears. After I had covered a hundred yards, I stopped and listened. There were noises ahead—high-pitched yips and yells. So they were on the beach. I began running again, and in a minute I rounded the bend, and there they were, maybe a quarter of a mile farther along. They had backed Handy into the water. The four males and two subadults had formed a semicircle around him at the water's edge, and were beginning to stone him. Handy was holding a rock in each hand, but he was not throwing. He would have to fumble in the water for stones, and he was not going to waste the ones he had on aimless throwing as the australopithecines were doing. I ran down the beach. "Ka," I shouted. "Ka."

The australopithecines turned to look, and taking advantage of it, Handy threw one of the rocks. It smacked off the head of one of the australopithecines with a sound I could hear all the way down the beach, and he collapsed to the sand and knelt there, holding his head. I charged on. I had never in my life hurt anybody before, never even hit anybody. I drew my spear back over my head like a baseball bat and then I was down on them. I closed my eyes and swung. I felt the spear bang on something and heard the flat splatting sound and a ring of shouts. I opened my eyes. Two of the australopithecines were on the ground and the other four were dancing off down the beach, shrieking and hollering. I gave Handy the spear and unslung my electro-prod. Instantly, Handy raised the spear to ram it through one of the australopithecines on the ground. I grabbed his arm. "Tee-ka," I shouted. Then I gestured and we ran toward the other four. They turned for a moment to face us, chattering and waving their fists, and then they broke and ran. In a moment they had disappeared into the tall grass. We swung around. The other two were on their feet and staggering off toward the grass farther along the beach. Handy started to run toward them, determined to kill somebody to get revenge, but again I grabbed his arm and we stood together on the beach as they, too, disappeared into the savannah grass.

Handy threw his arm upward. "Maymo," he shouted.

I grinned. I felt pretty good at winning something for a change. "Maymo, Handy," I said.

He threw his arms around me and hugged me. "Gar," he said. "Maymo, gar."

"Gar, Handy," I said.

"Gar," he said. And suddenly I realized that now he might tell me what I wanted to know. "Weddy," I said. "Doy Weddy."

He jerked away from me as if I had hit him, his forehead wrinkled over his protruding eyebrow ridges. He shook his head, as if he were trying to drive away an annoying fly. "Tee-doy," he said, looking away from me.

He was torn, I could see that. I grabbed him firmly by the arm, and stepped in front of him to force him to meet my eyes. "Gar," I said. "Doy Weddy."

He met my gaze, and then he looked down at the ground. "Tee-doy," he said, almost in a whisper. He was ashamed of himself, I was sure of that.

"Weddy gar," I said, once again. "Doy Weddy."

He looked around, licking his lips nervously, as if afraid that somebody was watching him. Then he said, "Doy Weddy." He turned abruptly and limped into the tall savannah grass.

13.

They had the Johers in a little animal skin hut set in the middle of a low ledge—really just a stone outcropping that rose a few feet above the level of the savannah. Handy and I crouched in the shadows of a grove of acacia trees about a half mile away, looking at it. In the distance the hut looked like a heap of animal skins. I figured it was made like the windbreak we had seen in the riverbed campsite—a circle of thorn branches with the skins flung over them, and probably supported in the middle by some kind of stick, or maybe a small heap of stones. The hut wasn't very high—about three feet, I guessed—and you would have to crawl on your hands and knees to get in and out.

I couldn't see the Johers—they were probably inside.

But I could see two habilines, both equipped with heavy sticks, sitting on the ledge by the opening to the hut.

Handy pointed. "Weddy," he said. He looked nervously around: He was plainly worried that somebody from his tribe would spot him in an act of treachery. They would probably kill him for it, I guessed. "Weddy," he said again, and began to back off on his hands and knees deeper into the woods. He was clearly eager to get away. He had helped me as much as he dared and would go no farther.

I wished I knew the Habilese word for "thanks," but I didn't. "Gar," I said. I crept back to him, and touched him on the shoulder. "Gar."

But he didn't respond. He was frowning, worried. He felt guilty about what he had done. Poor Handy, I thought. He had felt ashamed at not helping us, and now he felt guilty for helping. He couldn't win either way. The best favor I could do for him would be to let him go. So I squeezed his shoulder and said, "Gar," once more, and then I turned, and crawled back to the edge of the acacia forest. There I turned and looked back. Handy was up, limping through the shadowy woods as fast as he could. He didn't look back. I watched him for a moment, feeling sad that I would never see him again. But I had other things to worry about, and I turned back to face once more the little prison hut on the outcropping across the savannah grass.

I didn't know if I could take on two habilines equipped with clubs by myself. One lucky swing of a club and they might knock me down, or smash the prod, or knock it out of my hands, or something. I had the spear, too, but that would not be enough against two men attacking me from two sides.

But at night, if I took them by surprise, and if I could hand the spear in to Nuell, and they all came charging out—it might work. So I sat by the edge of the acacia forest watching and waiting in the heat and dust of the savannah as the sun went slowly down the sky. And out there everywhere in that grassy sea were animals: small herds of hipparions, pygmy giraffes, giant water buffalo, zebras, and once a little pack of huge gigantopithecines moving slowly along.

Finally, the sun went down, and night came on, pooling in the low place and then rising into the sky. I wanted to move before the first moon came up, and as soon as I could no longer make out the outline of the two habilines against the rock outcropping, I stepped out into the grass, bending low, and began to move through it in a long circle around the outcropping. It took me an hour to circle around to the back side, but I made it. I knelt there in the grass. Just ahead it thinned out, and then ended altogether, as the rocky ledge rose up out of it, like a little island in the sea. I sat and looked and listened. By now the first of Pleisto's moons had come up over the horizon and was lighting the savannah. I could see the rough lumps in the outcropping, and the little hut on top of it, quite clearly. Once I came out of the grass and started up the outcropping, I would be pretty easy to spot if the habilines happened to look down the back side of the ridge. I listened. All I could hear was the heavy thumping of my heart in my chest. Then I noticed the rim of the second moon coming over the horizon, and I decided I had better move before it got lighter still.

I checked the prod, which was slung over my back, and then I came out of the grass, carrying the spear in my right hand for readiness and using my left to grab onto the rock. The ridge was not steep. I could have walked up it easily enough, but I came up at a low crouch, using my left hand for support and trying to keep the point of the spear from clinking on the rock. Up I went, stopping every few feet to listen, and then suddenly I was right against the rear of the hut. I listened again. I could hear the sound of quiet breathing coming from inside. They were sleeping, but I guessed that one of them would be awake and on guard.

Gingerly, I touched the animal skin covering. It gave a little, and I figured there must be branches underneath holding the skins up. I took a deep breath, feeling my hands tremble a little. Then I stood, and with my free hand grabbed at one of the animal skins on top of the hut and gave it a jerk. At the same time I shouted, "Nuell, Nuell, grab the spear." There was a ripping noise as the skin dragged across the thorn branches. I flung it aside. "Grab the spear, Nuell."

A shout came from the front of the hut and a scrambling noise, as the habilines leaped to their feet. In front of me a figure came up into the moonlight out of the hole in the hut where I'd torn the skin away. It was Nuell. "Take the spear," I shouted. He grabbed it and I unslung the prod, and then the two habilines came charging through the bright moonlight toward me, their clubs upraised, their teeth bared in snarls. I leaped backward, half stumbling on the rough, rocky surface of the ledge. Nuell swung the spear around like a club. It cracked loudly on a habiline's skull and he dropped flat. The other habiline turned to face Nuell. I lunged forward with the prod. He shrieked as it touched his skin. Nuell jabbed with the spear, catching him in the ribs, and in a moment he was gone, racing away down the rock outcropping and into the tall grass. I knelt over the one Nuell had knocked down. He was lying flat on his face, moaning. He was breathing, but he seemed to be unconscious. Suddenly, Weddy and the professor and Nuell were around me. In the moonlight, I could see that Nuell was grinning. "Maymo, Char," he said.

14 ·

It took us all day and all the next to return to the spaceship. We spent the night on the little island where we'd fought the australopithecines and by the middle of the afternoon we were safely back. We were about as hungry as we'd ever been and we ate two days' supply of food and slept.

But with all the excitement my mind was churning around and around, and just at dusk I woke up. I lay there for a while, and when I realized that I couldn't sleep any more, I got up and went out into the pilot room. Professor Joher was there, dictating into his automatic typewriter, his lanky form bent over the microphone. As he talked in his rapid voice, he ran his hand through his gray hair. "I wanted to get some of this stuff down before it gets away from me, Char," he said.

"I guess I should write up my notes, too," I said.

"There's so much material, Char. A treasure trove. It'll take years just to begin to understand these hominids. The language alone could occupy a scholar for a lifetime."

"Once people can communicate with them, we'll be able to get a lot of other stuff."

"Yes," Professor Joher said. "But you have to be extremely cautious about putting ideas into their heads. You don't want to start teaching them concepts they don't possess. What ideas do they have about time, for example? Are they like animals, living mainly in an eternal present, or do they have some sense of a past and a future? Do they understand the inevitability of death? Do they have any rudimentary religion? Do they have rituals—do they celebrate a birth with a feast or a dance, for example? Do they believe in magic? You would have to go into all of this sort of thing very carefully, so as not to suggest foreign ideas to them."

"I think they might have an idea of time. I mean, they knew if they waited long enough the deinotherium would die. They must have experienced the same thing before and remembered it."

Professor Joher nodded. "Yes, that's suggestive. What else occurs to you, Char?"

I had been standing up, but I sat down at the table with him. That was the thing I liked best—being with

Professor Joher and just talking over scientific problems. "Well, the violence, mostly. We fought the australopithecines twice, the ramapithecines tried to kill Handy and that other group of habilines drove us out of the campsite. That's four battles in three days. It seems like a lot to me."

"Not much different from modern hominids, are they?" the professor said, smiling. "But I'll tell you something interesting, Char. Of all the nearly two hundred primate species, the two with the worst reputation for violence are the gorilla and the human being. Yet in fact, the reputation is all wrong. Gorillas are extremely peaceful animals. They may rise up roaring and pounding their chests in a typical threat gesture, but they hardly ever fight among themselves. They generally won't attack humans either, unless they're molested. People who have studied them in their natural surroundings have been able to come up quite close to them for hours at a time."

"But human beings are always at war. There's hardly been a time in history when there hasn't been a war going on somewhere."

"Yes, that's true, Char," he said. "But compared to what goes on in other primate bands, there's relatively little violence among us. If you look at, say, rhesus monkeys or langurs, you'll find an astonishingly large amount of friction in their daily lives. There's competitive pushing and shoving going on all the time, which sometimes breaks out into vicious battles that can result in serious wounding or even death. We human beings are no doubt just as competitive as other primates, but for the most part we control it better. Instead of getting into fistfights all the time, we compete in business or sports or politics or in climbing the social ladder. Look at Nuell and yourself, Char. The two of you are very competitive with each other, but you've never turned it into a physical battle, at least as far as I'm aware."

"No," I said. I was embarrassed and I blushed. "I guess we've never had a real fight."

"The two of you compete intellectually, by trying to outsmart each other or get the most praise."

I kept on blushing. It was true. "I guess I am sort of jealous of Nuell."

The professor shrugged. "That's natural," he said. "A pair of boys your age living together are bound to compete. I wouldn't worry about it. The main thing is to be aware of it. Don't try to pretend it isn't there. The only way you can keep control of it is to recognize it."

That made me feel better. "I guess I didn't want to recognize it," I said.

"But you can see, can't you, if you and Nuell get into arguments, why these hominids on Pleisto might fight. Surely there were times when you were angry enough at Nuell to want to hit out at him. You didn't, because we humans are equipped with powerful social regulations against that sort of thing. It's understandable that in less well-developed hominids like the habilines, the fighting will break through more frequently."

"What I noticed was that the fighting was mostly

between different groups," I said. "Each group didn't fight among itself so much."

"Aha. Char, you've put your finger right on it. That's the whole point. We may compete *within* our own groups, but we try to keep the conflicts within bounds, so that nobody actually gets hurt. I mean, if you and Nuell get into a little argument, nobody pays much attention. But if you began to shout and holler at the dinner table, somebody would eventually step in, because you'd be disrupting things for the rest of us. And if you grabbed up knives, or started wrestling around on the floor where you might damage the furniture or hurt somebody else, the rest of us would immediately put a stop to it. Groups of hominids control internal violence. But against other groups, it's another story. We see them as outsiders, as strangers, as 'them,' and we feel free to do almost anything we want to them. Handy could attack the australopithecines without thinking twice about it, but he didn't want to go against his own people even to the point of helping us to escape. It was only when you saved his life that he knew he had to do it."

Something was occurring to me. "So there are two sides to it then—the friendly side and the hostile side."

Professor Joher ran his hand through his sparse hair and gazed out the window for a moment. Then he said, "In the past three days you observed four incidents of serious battling. But how many examples of friendship, affection, concern for others did you see?"

I stopped to think. "Well, Handy helped us to escape."

He stared at me. "And *you* helped us to escape, too. That was a big risk for you. You didn't have to do it."

I felt embarrassed. "Well, it was all of us trying to find you," I said.

"Yes," he said. "That, too. And Weddy taking care of Handy's foot. And you all saving Handy from the ramapithecines. And you and Nuell trying to protect all of you from the smilodon. And Handy bringing the nuts to Weddy. And—well, it would make a very long list."

I scratched my head. "I never thought about it that way," I said. "All I could see was the violence—the competing."

"I think that's the way we all are. We see the violence because it troubles us. And there's no way around it—human beings are competitive animals. But we're also cooperative, loving, kind, generous, nurturing, protective, self-sacrificing—we're all those things, too. Just think how much of your ordinary daily life you spend working with other people, or doing things for them. It'll amaze you when you start to add it up. Well,"—he glanced at his watch—"we'd better get some sleep. We've got a lot of planning to do tomorrow. We've got to figure out what our next step is."

I stared at him, my mouth dropping open. "You mean we're not going back to earth?"

"Certainly not right away, Char. With an opportunity for discovery like this at hand? Char, you're going to spend your life studying these hominids. If you do your work well, you're going to become one of the most famous scientists of your day."

A chill rose up my back. I wanted to fall on Professor Joher and hug him, but I couldn't. Professor Joher stood. He put his arm around my shoulder and gave me a little squeeze. "Let's go to bed," he said. It was good enough for me.

HOW MUCH OF
THIS BOOK IS TRUE? •

There is, of course, no planet named Pleisto. In fact, we do not know today of any planet that resembles earth closely enough to support life as we have it here. Some scientists believe that such planets must exist just on the odds; but others say that the development of life on earth through millions upon millions of years of evolution has been so rare a phenomenon that it could not have happened twice.

However, what I have tried to do in this book is to give as accurate a picture as I could of Pleistocine times in East Africa, where it is thought that humans first made their appearance. We are only just beginning to understand these early creatures and their environment.

However, in the past decade we have filled in large gaps in our understanding of early humans.

We currently believe that the primate line originated in the closing days of the dinosaur era, perhaps a hundred million years ago, with a small animal called a tree shrew. By about thirty million years ago there had evolved a variety of monkeys and apes. Most of these lived in trees, but eventually certain apes began to live mainly on the ground. The human line is thought to have evolved from one of these terrestrial apes.

The transition from ape to humanlike types occurred at least five million years ago. There were apparently several of these hominids at one time or another, among them the kinds mentioned in this book. One of them was *Homo habilis*, the "handy man" central to the story. It is today widely believed that the human line descends from *Homo habilis*.

Like virtually all primates, they lived in groups. They were very social creatures. There were leaders and followers, friends and enemies, just as we have in our own groups today. Whether they paired off as we do in marriage, or mated randomly, as other primates do, we cannot say.

They made their living through a mixed economy. That is to say, they ate almost anything edible around them: snails, fish, birds, turtles, eggs, shellfish, snakes, roots, berries, nuts and possibly grain. What proportion of their living came from hunting we do not know. Most probably they were able to bring down an occasional antelope or similar animal, usually the young, aged or injured. They may have scavenged by driving wild dogs or cats off their kill.

To thus earn their living, they were capable of making a wide variety of tools from stone—small chips with sharp edges that they could use to cut through tendons, bigger choppers for hacking the kill apart, and various pointed and knifelike ones for skinning and other tasks. We also presume that they made tools of bone and wood because if they could shape stone, we think they would certainly have figured out how to shape softer materials. We have the remains of some bones which may or may not have been used as clubs, or prises, but of course all of these wooden tools have disappeared. It is probable that they made spears, as suggested in this story. They did not have fire and would not have used the burn-and-scrape method that Char employed to make his spear. They would have scraped out a point with a stone tool.

They also, it seems clear from various finds, built shelters by sticking branches into the ground, propping them up with heaps of stones and covering them with skins or hides. Whether they used hides as cloaks as well we can only guess. They did not, we are fairly sure, possess the ability to sew or weave, make pottery or baskets, make rope and tie knots, carve out a boat or build anything other than a pile of stones. Their skills were rudimentary, limited, and learned painfully over millions of years. We can see how hard won was this early knowledge by noting that at some periods their stone tools did not improve for a million years at a stretch. Yet these techniques vastly outreached anything else in the animal world, and they were the foundation on which humankind built our dominance of the world. But in the end, perhaps the most important of the human skills were not technical, but social. The human ability to intermesh a series of diverse operations into a larger whole has been of overriding importance in our development. For human beings, *cooperation* is the name of the game.

This sort of cooperation, with divisions of labor in which various members of the group do different tasks for the common good, cannot exist without a system of communication. Virtually all types of animals, including insects, have signal systems—the familiar songs of birds, the dance of the honey bees, growls of dogs.

In the higher primates—the so-called great apes, which include gorillas, chimpanzees and the orangutans —there are quite clear facial gestures. In humans we call these facial "expressions," which can be easily understood. Many of these gestures have been inherited by us in modified form. For example, the human smile descends from what is termed the "fear grimace" in a number of other primates, in which the lips are pulled back and the teeth bared. The fear grimace exists in other primates to show a disinclination to fight. Our smile, used to show friendliness, is much the same thing. For example, when we are introduced to a stranger, we are likely to smile to show that we are not hostile or threatening.

The great apes also have many vocalizations to show their feelings and intentions. They whimper, growl, shriek to indicate one mood or another. But whether they are capable of true language is a point of much contention in the scientific world today. Experiments have clearly shown that chimpanzees can use symbols to communicate with human beings. Chimpanzees have been taught to ask for chocolate or oranges, to go out to play and many other things, by using hand signals, or markers of one kind of another. Indeed, domestic animals like dogs and horses will respond to verbal signals like "Sit!" or "Whoa!"

But many experimenters do not believe that this sort of communication constitutes true language. They contend only human beings have real language. The question that then arises is whether the early hominids had language and if so, what kind. We are pretty sure that they would have had some signaling system more advanced than what we see in chimpanzees, but one that was certainly less complex and expressive than ours.

But what was it? We really don't know. In the book you have just read I have made my own guess. I have created for Handy a rudimentary language made up of a set of cries or "words" for what I feel to be the most important things Handy had to communicate: "watch out," "friend," "foe" and the like. On the basis of what we know about chimpanzees, we can be fairly certain that he must have had some system of vocalization of this kind.

However, I have also given Handy a rudimentary syntax in the possession of a negative. This is more speculative. It is one thing for a species to develop a simple one-to-one relationship between a symbol and an object; that is, the word "tree" stands for the real tree we see in the park. It is quite another thing to have enough brain power to grasp a concept like "opposite," or "good." The word "tree" stands for one sort of thing. The concept of "opposite" applies to many things: the opposite of cold is hot, the opposite of up is down, and so forth. Thus, while we suspect that these early hominids may have possessed a rudimentary set of symbols for things and acts that were important to them, we cannot be at all sure that they were capable of understanding concepts like "negative" and "positive."

For the same reason, we cannot be sure that they would have been able to work out a system of taking prisoners, as I have given the habilines in this book. They may have; they may not. We also are not sure that they would have been able to kill large animals like a deinotherium by driving them into swamps and gradually wearing them down.

However, it does seem fairly likely that hominids were able to do most of the other things I have given them to do in this book, such as driving strangers out of a campsite with threat gestures and a shower of stones. We are also fairly confident that they had a division of

labor between the sexes, with the males doing the dangerous tasks like hunting and fighting. If the tribe was to go
on existing, the females and offspring were simply too
valuable to risk in dangerous activities. It has always
been true of primates that the males are expendable.

Which brings us to the main question this book is
asking: Did these early primates fight, and if so, why?
We have no direct evidence that they did, but I believe
it is almost certainly true. Jane Goodall, who has devoted
her life to studying chimpanzees in the Gombe Stream
region of Tanzania, witnessed a real war between two
chimpanzee groups that resulted in the destruction of
one of them. Of all the several thousands of human cul-
tures studied, from the most primitive to the most ad-
vanced, only a tiny handful could be described as truly
peaceful, and these for the most part were small groups
that had a great deal to lose by starting a war with a
larger neighbor. Furthermore, in virtually all primate
species, groups are hostile to one another. They do not
often fight when they meet, but they will fight in certain
circumstances, for example, when one group finds another one sleeping in a tree it considers its own.

It seems, therefore, that intergroup hostility is a
fact of primate life and that includes humankind. Why?
What's it all about? Several theories have been offered.
One says that primate species are by nature "territorial."
Each group has its piece of ground that it will defend
against intruders. But in fact, primates frequently have

overlapping ranges and will share water holes and the like.

Human beings are not territorial either. Wars are usually fought *on* land, but they are mostly not *about* it. You might consider the reasons behind the Arab-Israeli War, the American Civil War, or World War II. You will note that at the conclusion of each, the victors gave most of the conquered land back to the losers.

Another theory says that people—males especially —have an innate "aggressive drive" which they have to express in competitive sports, arguing, or fighting from time to time. It does seem true that in all primates, including humans, the males tend to compete to get to the top of their heaps. But for reasons too technical to go into here, there are good arguments against the aggressive drive theory. It seems more likely that people will fight when there is something to fight about —the defense of the tribe, or gold or a trade advantage —but that they don't fight unnecessarily.

Why, then, do we have wars? Part of it, I am certain, has to do with the intergroup hostility which I have shown in this book. We are horrified by the idea of murdering a member of our own group. We are less horrified when it is a foreigner, and even less when it is a member of another species. Once two groups find themselves in conflict over something, even something minor like a campsite, they begin to push and shove until actual fighting breaks out. Groups, even when they are outnumbered, do not easily back down. Once friction starts, the conflict tends to escalate rather than die down.

However, whether this is the correct answer or not is something I hope that future students of the human being will determine. The question, surely, is one well worth pondering.